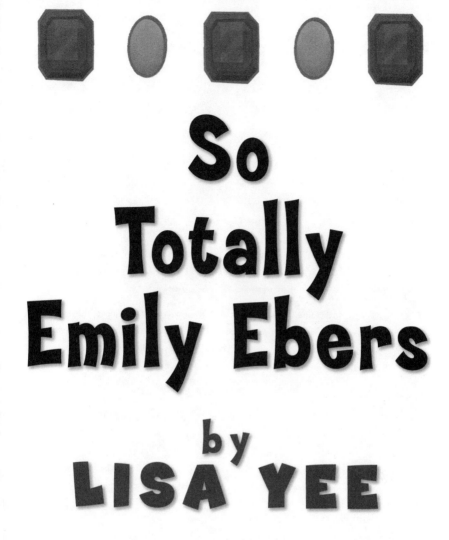

So Totally Emily Ebers

by LISA YEE

ARTHUR A. LEVINE BOOKS
An Imprint of Scholastic Inc.

Text copyright © 2007 by Lisa Yee.

All rights reserved. Published by Arthur A. Levine Books, an imprint of Scholastic Inc.,
Publishers since 1920. SCHOLASTIC and the LANTERN LOGO are trademarks and/or
registered trademarks of Scholastic Inc.

Library of Congress Cataloging-in-Publication Data

Yee, Lisa.

So totally Emily Ebers / by Lisa Yee. — 1st ed.

p.   cm.

Summary: In a series of letters to her absent father, twelve-year-old Emily Ebers deals with
moving cross-country, her parents' divorce, a new friendship, and her first serious crush.

ISBN-13: 978-0-439-83847-4

ISBN-10: 0-439-83847-9

[1. Moving, Household—Fiction. 2. Friendship—Fiction. 3. Divorce—Fiction. 4. Parent
and child—Fiction. 5. California—Fiction. 6. Letters—Fiction.] I. Title.

PZ7.Y3638So 2007   [Fic]—dc22   2006022738

Book design by Elizabeth B. Parisi

10 9 8 7 6 5 4 3 2 1   07 08 09 10 11

Printed in the United States of America
First edition, April 2007

This book is dedicated to
Marieke and Kate,
and to best friends everywhere.

JUNE 7

Dear Dad,

Today was the last day of school and the second saddest day of my entire life. A.J. and Nicole were crying and crying, and I was crying, and then Mrs. Buono started crying. This freaked everyone out because teachers aren't supposed to cry. My whole class had made me a humongous card, and everyone wrote nice things, even Evan. When I finished reading it, I began bawling and Nicole started wheezing so badly that Mrs. Buono was convinced she was having another asthma attack. A.J. and I offered to take Nicole to the nurse.

We managed to wait until we were halfway down the hall to begin laughing hysterically.

When we could breathe again, A.J. brought up the time we were in first grade and Mr. Kinnoin won the lottery. He climbed up on his desk and shouted, "Okay, you little weenies, you're never going to see me in a classroom again!" Then he burst into tears and ran out of the room.

Nicole reminded us how in second grade we dressed as the three little pigs for Halloween, and whenever anyone asked us anything, we'd just make piggy noises. Then I remembered when A.J.'s hamster died and we had a funeral for her, and then we all started crying all over again.

It's after midnight now. The house is empty. The movers came today. When I got home from school, Mom was trailing them around shouting, "That's fragile!" and "Do you have any idea what it would cost to replace that?!?!" She's conked out in a sleeping bag next to the fireplace, still clutching her clipboard. I guess yelling at moving men is exhausting.

I'd better get to bed too. Tomorrow's going to be rough. I wish you were here to sing me to sleep like you used to do when I was little. I packed my Elmo tape recorder in a box labeled "Emily's Most Important Things." It has the cassette of you singing "The Emily Song" in it. That's the first thing I'm going to unpack when we get to California.

Good night, Daddy.

Love,

Emily

JUNE 8

Dear Dad,

I can't believe we had to say good-bye. This is the second saddest day of my life. (I'm moving yesterday to the third saddest day of my life. Even though yesterday was bad, today was really, really bad, like rip-your-heart-out-and-stomp-on-it bad.) When we hugged I never wanted to let you go.

Do you still have Mom's cell phone number? I know you had to write it on your hand when I gave it to you. I hope you didn't accidentally wash it off. I know you're not a phone person, but you should know how to reach us in case of an emergency. What about the malted milk balls I gave you? Are they all gone now? I'll bet they are! And did you notice that I wrote our California address inside the card I made for you? I also wrote it on all those address labels to make it easy for you to write to me. Only if you want to, of course.

Did you cry when we said good-bye? I think I saw you cry. I know I was crying. After you drove off, I pulled up the FOR SALE sign in the front yard and hid it behind the garage. It was a lot heavier than I thought it would be. When Mom found out, I got in big trouble.

"EMILY LAURA EBERS . . . how could you . . . ?"

She never did finish her sentence.

As Mom backed out of the driveway and we took off, I turned around to watch our house get smaller and smaller. I said good-bye to Mrs. Metz's lawn gnomes, and to the S. Cockroft Memorial Library, and to Twoheys. I said good-bye to the Town Clock, and to Crestwood Lake, and to the Celery Farm.

I said good-bye to Allendale, New Jersey.

After a while, I didn't recognize where we were, so I stopped saying good-bye to everything and just zoned out.

"Shall we play the license-plate game?" Mom asked.

Huh? I had forgotten she was there. The sight of her gripping the steering wheel was so irritating I wanted to scream. *Why can't she be a more laid-back driver like you?* I didn't answer her stupid question about the stupid license-plate game, and she seemed to just forget she had asked. We didn't talk at all. Not when we had lunch at McDonald's, or when she went the wrong way on the turnpike, or when we checked into some motel in Pennsylvania at night. I didn't even beg her to let me swim in the pool.

I can't believe she's doing this to us. Every mile we drive is a mile farther away from you. That's why this letter journal is so important. It's like I'm writing you letters that you'll get all at once. I got the idea from Mrs. Buono when she told the class to keep a journal over the summer. I thought, instead of writing "Dear Diary," why not write "Dear Dad"? I know you're traveling and super-busy, but you can read it when summer's over and you have more time. Then you'll know what I've been up to and you won't have to worry about me.

At our last stop, I bought a pack of gum, some peanut brittle, and a map of the United States. When we get to California, I'm going to put the map on my wall and mark all the places you will be visiting during your Talky Boys comeback tour. That way I can keep track of you. I wish, I wish, I wish I could be on the road with you instead of Mom. But I know. You told me, "Life on the road is tough when you're in a band." I totally believe it. It's torture being here with Mom and we're not even trying to sing or harmonize or anything. I hate her.

Love,
Emily

JUNE 9

Dear Dad,

It seems like every ten miles Mom pulls off to the side of the road and consults her maps and her AAA auto club books. She's put Post-its on every page. "I think this side trip will be worth it, don't you?" she asks, without waiting for my answer, and then she turns off the road for another sleep-inducing museum.

This is not a trip, it's a bore-Emily-to-death ride. Only Mom calls it "A&E's Americana Adventure." Overnight she's gone from mute to nonstop yakking. She keeps saying, "This is so fun. Isn't this fun?"

Uh. No.

I'm glad TB is riding in the car with me. Mom says that I'm a little old to be dragging around a teddy bear, but I don't care. TB is my friend and he needs me.

Yesterday at the Johnny Appleseed Museum, some grungy barefoot guy wearing a name tag reading "Johnny A." came up to me, said, "Welcome to Ohio!" and offered me an apple. I didn't take it. Later, Mom said I was rude. I was not rude. I'm just not an apple person, okay? If I ate one, choked, and spit it up, *that* would be rude.

To make up for my "lack of consideration," Mom made a big deal about joining the Johnny Appleseed Society. Then when Johnny A. offered her a complimentary basket of apples, she said, "Oh! They look lovely," and proceeded to talk to him about apples for AN HOUR. Luckily, there was a honey exhibit nearby, and I passed the time by staring at the bees trapped between two panes of glass. I knew how they felt.

This afternoon, Mom kept singing, "Get your kicks on Route 66!" It wasn't funny the first time she sang it, so why would she think I'd want to hear it seven hundred more times? When we stopped at the Amish Interpretive Center in Illinois, Mom started running around the gift shop in her gray velour tracksuit with an Amish bonnet stuck on her head.

"Here, Emily, you try one on!"

I wrapped myself up in a quilt and ignored her.

How did the pioneers do it? Did they have to ride with their mothers? There's no way I'm going to make it to California.

Love,

Emily

JUNE 12

Hey Dad,

So get this. We're in Missouri at the Museum of Independent Telephone Pioneers, and Mom grabs one of the old-fashioned phones and "calls" me. When I wouldn't pick up, she pokes me and says, "Emily, answer the phone!"

Why? Why should I answer the phone when she's standing right next to me? The museum was Mom's idea of a good time. A building full of clunky telephones the size of cash registers. Fascinating.

Do you think you'll ever get a cell phone again? Are you having a better time now that you're "out of the rat race"? Wait. Don't answer. Dumb question. Of course you are. Everyone knows you hated selling houses. I'm glad your band decided to reunite. Maybe someday, Nicole and A.J. and I will reunite. Maybe you and Mom will too. Just a thought.

The Boot Hill Museum in Kansas was much better than the telephone museum. I liked looking at the old posters of outlaws. Some of them were actually kind of cute. I wonder what it would be like to have a cowboy boyfriend. Would he take me to the mall on a horse? Would he wear his hat in a movie theater? Would he pay for dinner with gold nuggets?

Mom and I drank sarsaparillas and she even bought me a purple cowboy hat. When I'm not wearing it, TB uses it as a bed. Later we stopped at Central City Ghost Town in Colorado. We walked around the cemetery and I read all of the grave markers. It was fun in a creepy sort of way. Some families all died at the same time. Others died on different dates but were buried near each other. Lots of people were buried alone.

"Did you ever wish we had a big family, Emily?" Mom asked.

"I never thought about it," I lied. I've always wanted a sister.

"I've often wondered what it would have been like if you had a sibling. Maybe things would have been easier for you."

I didn't ask what she meant. I was too busy looking

at the graves and wondering where I would be buried now. In New Jersey? In California? Near you? Near Mom?

Alone?

Love,

Emily

JUNE 14

Hi Dad,

Even with all of her maps and schedules and checklists, Mom keeps getting lost. It's not like her. Usually she knows exactly where she's going. Still, even when it's clear we're lost, Mom just plows ahead and pretends like nothing is wrong. She's gotten really good at pretending.

Mom and I have finally found a system that seems to work well for both of us. During the day, I sleep while she drives, and at night she sleeps while I watch television or read my Betty & Veronica comics in the motel. The only time we're both awake is when Mom drags me to see museums and monuments, or when we're eating. Patty (that's what I call Mom's car) looks like a dumpster and smells like rotting apples. Mom doesn't keep her car clean like you do. It is so great that you have the same kind of car that one of the Beatles had. Remember when you got that car? It was right after the divorce was final. You said, "Emily, you can pick the color."

And I said, "Purple!"

"Purple? I thought you'd pick red."

"I like red too," I told you. And that's how Spidey (that's what I've named your car) got to be red.

So today, Mom and I were arguing over who ate the last Mint Milano when suddenly we both gasped. Right smack in front of us was the Grand Canyon. It was the most amazing thing I've ever seen. Mom slowed Patty down. (Normally she speeds, so this was significant.)

"Over 1,200,000 acres," she whispered.

I had a hard time imagining that. But then, math is my worst subject. After refueling at the snack bar, Mom and I hiked up a trail. It looked like it went on forever. As usual, she was acting weird and kept asking how I was feeling. Finally we stopped to rest at a shady place under a tree. The view was amazing.

"Honey, I know the divorce has been difficult for you," she began as she sat down on a rock. "But in time you'll see it's for the best." I didn't answer. Instead, I just watched her making circles in the dirt with a twig. "I've been doing a lot of thinking," she continued, "and I've come to a big decision."

I looked up. Maybe we were going to turn around and head home. Maybe I was on a hidden-camera television show and this was all just some sort of joke.

"What is it?" I held my breath.

"Well, you're getting older . . ." She hesitated before blurting out, "I think it's time you called me 'Alice'!"

"Alice???"

"Yes?"

"You want me to call you by your first name?"

"I want us to be closer. Perhaps you'll feel more comfortable calling me Alice. Maybe we can be friends." She looked pleased with herself.

"Alice . . ."

She leaned forward and brushed the bangs from her eyes. For the first time I noticed gray hiding in her brown hair. Her hair's too long for a mom. "Yes, Emily, what is it you want to tell me?"

"Alice, you're sitting on a pile of ants."

As Mom — I mean *Alice* — hopped around, I walked to the edge of the cliff. The Grand Canyon seemed to go on forever. There was a rail to keep people from falling, or jumping, or throwing someone off. I considered all three.

Tomorrow I see our new house. I'll bet it's going to be really ugly. It makes me sad to think of you in your cramped little apartment. You call it a "studio." I call it a shoebox. Even though you have your own place, I sort of thought that maybe you'd move back to our Allendale house. You could even turn my room into a music studio. I really don't think we should sell the house. Will you at least think about it?

Love,
Emily

JUNE 15

Dear Daddy,

We finally, finally arrived in Rancho Rosetta, California, just as the sun was setting.

Our house looks like it could be in a magazine. It's huge! My new room is big enough for me to do two cartwheels in it. Plus, there's a *walk-in closet*. Our stuff hasn't arrived yet, which is too bad. I think it would be fun to ride my bike through the house.

Alice's master bedroom has a Jacuzzi in the bathroom, and my room connects to *my own bathroom*! There's a ton of counter space and the bathtub is really deep. TB and I are sitting in it at this very moment, but there's no water. That gets turned on tomorrow. Right now my room is white, but Alice says I can paint it. It will be purple, what else?

Alice has claimed the spare room for her office. The den would be perfect for air hockey or the pool table you've always wanted, but when I brought it up, Alice just scratched the ant bites on her leg and stared off into space. This house is so much bigger than the one in Allendale. I'm not sure why we need so much space. The backyard is smaller than our old one, though. I really miss our backyard and how it just seemed to go on forever into the woods. I haven't seen any deer here, but there are plenty of palm trees, just like you'd imagine they'd have in southern California. We even have one in the front yard!

Today we explored the town. It's sort of like Allendale, where you can walk everywhere, except here there are lots of new stores and restaurants mixed in with funky old ones, and you wouldn't believe how clean it all is. There's this brand-new Super Target with everything in the world in it including — get this — sushi. And there's Benny's Doughnut Palace where you can decorate your own doughnuts. Plus, all the cars look new and everyone's lawn is green like a television commercial.

For dinner tonight we went to this place called Stout's Coffee Shop. It sort of reminds me of Twoheys, with red booths, checkered tablecloths with glass over them, and plastic covering the menus. I ordered blueberry pancakes, hash browns, and eggs over easy, in your honor. I wanted to order black coffee too, but Alice wouldn't let me. I didn't tell her that whenever you took me to Twoheys, you always let me sip your coffee. That's one of our secrets!

The waitress was really nice. She reminded me of A.J.'s Grandma Jane, except she had rings on every finger and a small butterfly tattoo on her arm.

"Do you have any questions?" Libby asked, motioning to the menu.

"Actually I do have a couple," Alice said, before launching into a billion questions about the town and the people and the city council. . . . Libby barely had time to answer before Alice asked her something else. I hate it that Alice is always prying. It's embarrassing. "I'm a journalist," she says. "It's my job."

Yeah, but 24/7?

"What do people like to do around here?" Alice reached for her second buttermilk biscuit. Stout's has the best biscuits.

"Well, there's a really nice mall." Libby smiled at me as she adjusted the hairnet over her bun. It looked like she had a giant chocolate doughnut on top of her head. "They just redid it. I'd hang out there myself, if I ever got any time off. And if you're into sports, basketball is big in this town. Does your daughter like volleyball? The girls' volleyball league is taking sign-ups right now."

"Emily's never been very athletic" — *gee, thanks, Alice* — "but people change, so you never know."

As Alice and Libby kept blabbering, I poked a hole in my eggs and watched the yolk ooze out. Could my life get any more boring?

I wonder what A.J. and Nicole did today. I'll bet they went to the movies and then to Twoheys for hot-fudge sundaes. I want to call them, but our phones still aren't hooked up, and Alice claims it's too expensive to use her cell phone because "roaming charges can really add up."

Now that I'm in Rancho Rosetta, it's finally hitting me that I won't see you until Thanksgiving. I don't know if I can wait that long. At least this letter journal is making me feel like we're still connected. I think about you all the time. I hope you think about me too.

Love,
Emily

JUNE 17

Hey Dad!

The movers arrived today, so I finally, finally, finally have furniture in my room. All that was in here before was my suitcase and the map of the United States on the wall. I put a red sticker on Allendale, New Jersey, since that's where we both left from — only you'll be returning at the end of summer.

TB and I are very happy to be sleeping in our own bed tonight. As usual, we are taking the top bunk. It's very private up here, plus we like the view.

Alice got all weirded out because some boxes are missing. "How can they just disappear? HOW CAN THEY JUST DISAPPEAR?!!!" She covered her mouth with both hands. "I am so sorry," she sobbed. "It's just that, I had everything so organized, they were numbered, and cataloged, I had lists . . . I'm sorry. I'm sorry. I'm sorry." The movers just walked away, shaking their heads. I felt totally humiliated.

It's boxes, boxes everywhere, except the box with her lists in it is missing. It will take us forever to find anything. Luckily, "Emily's Most Important Things" showed up. I checked to make sure everything was still there: my Elmo tape recorder, the photo of the three of us in the teacups at Disneyland, my baby blanket, Alice's big paisley scarf, your Members Only jacket, and that bottle of shiny rocks from the State Fair.

The first room Alice got all set up was her office. Well, not totally set up, but her desk looks exactly the same as it did in Allendale with her pens and paper and everything just so. That weird crystal flame she won last year is sitting on her bookshelf along with her ten billion other awards, and she's already working on her computer. What a surprise.

I asked her about e-mail again.

"No, Emily, we've been over this before."

"Well then, can I have my own computer?"

Alice did one of her famous sighs and stopped typing mid-word. "Not until you prove that you can be more responsible. You do know you are not to touch my computer, right?"

I can't believe she's still holding that against me. How was I to know that "Delete This" was an article about spam? I thought I was doing her a favor! Remember how hard you laughed? And when you said, "I've told you a million times, you need to back up your files," Alice locked herself in the bathroom for two hours. Well, at least now we each have our own bathroom.

"But if I had a computer, I could e-mail Dad and connect with A.J. and Nicole on OurSpace."

"Emily, you know your father sold his computer when he quit his job. And as for OurSpace, didn't you read that article I wrote about the dangers of the Internet?"

"Alice . . ."

"Not now, Emily. Not now."

If not now, then when?
XOXO,
EE

P.S. Guess what I listened to today? "The Emily Song"!
I kept playing it and rewinding, playing it and rewinding. When I play your song, it's like you're right here
next to me. I could listen to it all day!

JUNE 18

Dad,
HELP!!!

My life in Rancho Rosetta is over before it's even
begun. Alice has signed me up for volleyball!!! She knows
I hate sports, so that must mean she hates me.

"Emily, this will get you out of the house. You said
you wanted to meet people, plus the physical activity will
be good for you —"

"Right. I said I wanted to meet people, not make a
fool of myself trying to hit a ball over a net."

"Emily! This is not open to discussion. . . ."

I tuned her excuses out and tuned in to Mongo Bongo
in my head. I still can't believe you once opened for them.
They're like rock royalty, even though they're really old

now and look ridiculous wearing those shiny tight pants. I saw a documentary about them the other day on RockStar TV. Someday, they'll be doing a documentary about the Talky Boys! Ooooh, I hope they interview me. I'll say, "Dave 'the Dude' Ebers is the best singer in the entire world!!!"

How's your tour going? I'll bet you're getting tons and tons of new fans every time you take the stage. I told this to Alice last night, but she got all spazzed out and her lower lip started shaking. So I asked her about global warming and she calmed right down and launched into this brain-numbing lecture I couldn't understand. It really doesn't matter. I don't listen to Alice. When I tuned in to her rant again, I tried reasoning with her about this dumb volleyball thing, but she's so stubborn.

"Alice, volleyball just isn't my thing."

"Emily, it wouldn't hurt you to try something new."

"*Alice*, I am trying something new. I moved here, didn't I?"

"*Emily*, we all have to do things we don't want to do sometimes."

"*Alice*, why do I have to do things I don't want to do ALL THE TIME?"

Alice pushed her chair away from her desk. "*Emily*, there's no need to get hysterical."

"*ALICE*, I AM NOT BEING HYSTERICAL, I AM BEING HONEST! I DON'T WANT TO PLAY VOLLEYBALL, I DON'T WANT TO LIVE IN

RANCHO ROSETTA, I DON'T WANT TO BE
HERE AT ALL, AND IT'S ALL YOUR FAULT!!!"

"Emily! EMILY LAURA EBERS, you come back
right now. . . ."

I didn't wait to hear what Alice had to say. I wish you
were with me. Or I wish I were wherever you are. I wish
I were anywhere but here.

Love,
Emily

JUNE 20

Dearest Daddy,
MY OWN CREDIT CARD!!!

You do love me! Thank you, thank you, thank you,
thank you, thank you! Oh, and in case you hadn't
heard . . . THANK YOU!!! It's the best birthday present
ever. I was so thrilled when I got the mail and saw one of
my address labels on an envelope. The card was so cute,
an elephant driving a convertible! But then when I opened
it and a credit card fell out, I went into shock. You are the
greatest dad in the entire world!

Remember the time you showed up at my party in a
big black limo and whisked me and A.J. and Nicole and
everyone to Serendipity 3 in Manhattan? That was like a

total dream — especially when you ordered gigantic banana splits for EACH of us — but this is even better. My own credit card! I like that it's shiny and silver and has my name on it right in front. It's soooo official.

"A credit card?" Leave it to Alice to try to ruin everything. "Emily, aren't you a little young for a credit card?" she asked in a tone that said, "Because I think you are a little young for a credit card."

"Daddy doesn't think so."

"Yes, well, I think it's rather irresponsible of him to give you a credit card at your age. Besides, he can't even pay off his own credit-card bills. What's he doing giving one to you?"

"You're just saying that because he loves me and did something nice for me. You're just jealous!"

"Emily!" Alice shouted, before turning all red. "Your father is just . . . your father . . ."

She never did finish her sentence. Instead she retreated to her office.

Alice is so mean sometimes. It's like you used to say, "She just doesn't get it."

Well, I'm not letting Alice get in the way of my happiness, because it's my birthday and I have MY OWN CREDIT CARD. She was still locked in her office when I headed to the mall. Luckily everything in Rancho Rosetta is in walking distance. I'd rather pedal a tricycle around town than ask Alice for a ride anywhere.

The Rancho Rosetta Mall is two stories tall and has

three department stores, including a Shah's! When I neared the entrance, the doors parted and the air-conditioning washed over me. I grinned as I stepped inside. The stores looked so inviting. I know you said the card is only for emergencies, and maybe something small now and then, but MY OWN CREDIT CARD! Don't worry, I was careful not to max it out, plus I bought all practical stuff like a BeDazzler.

When I got home, Alice was hunched over her computer, typing away.

"Emily, there you are!" she said, straightening up. She had changed out of her blue tracksuit into that black LAYA skirt and cream Meriel Rohana blouse I like. "Come on, get dressed. We've got reservations!"

Alice was smiling and I was relieved that she had recovered from her temper tantrum. It's like Mood Swing Central around here.

We went to a fancy restaurant called Chavelaque. Because it was my birthday, I got to order whatever I wanted. I had three appetizers — shrimp cocktail, home-made potato chips, and some cheese thing that I didn't eat because I found out it was made with *goat* cheese. (Ewwwww!) At the end of dinner, the waitress brought out a small chocolate cake. All the servers stood around our table and started singing "Happy Birthday." Alice sang too (off-key as usual), and some people from the other tables joined in. Everyone stopped eating and looked at me. It was pretty neat. I wonder if this is how celebrities feel? Is this how you used to feel when your band was really, really famous?

"Blow out the candles," Alice said.

I squeezed my eyes shut and made a wish. Then I blew out the candles and everyone applauded. But when I opened my eyes, Alice was still sitting alone and you were nowhere to be seen.

When we got home, there were presents waiting for me on the kitchen table. Alice gave me a pair of really nice silver hoop earrings. They're hypoallergenic so I won't get an infection, like the last time I wore hoops. She also got me a prepaid phone card with $20 on it. Now I can call A.J. and Nicole. I'd call you too, but I don't know where you are. I wish your tour poster listed more than just the cities you'll be appearing in. It would be so cool for me to be able to keep track of you.

Nicole and A.J. sent me a framed photo of our last day at Wilcox Academy, and they also sent some really great metallic blue nail polish and the sweetest monkey wallet. I even got a card from Evan. Can you believe it? Ever since I broke off our engagement in kindergarten, he's sort of ignored me. I guess he's not so bad. And he is sort of cute, even if I am so much taller than him.

Overall, my birthday was pretty good, except when Alice got all teary-eyed because, "Emily, twelve years old, you're practically a teenager!" I only wish you could have been here. I'm getting better at pretending you are. If you can't find your aftershave, it's because I took it the last time

I visited you. Right before I started writing this letter, I had just put the cap back on when Alice came into my room.

"What's that smell?"

"Um, just a perfume sample from a magazine."

"Oh. It's just that it smells like . . . never mind. Nothing. It's time for bed, Emily. Good night, honey."

Well, it's really late. I'd better get to bed before Alice comes back and tells me to turn off the lights. Maybe next year we can all celebrate my birthday together. Thanks again for my credit card. It's the best gift anyone's ever given me.

Love always,
Your Birthday Girl

JUNE 21

Dear Dad,

I was in my room reading *Gamma Girl* magazine when Alice pushed the door open. She didn't even knock. She handed me a pair of shorts and a T-shirt. I opened my mouth to protest, but Alice cut me off. "Emily, please don't start," was all she said before leaving.

I stared at the volleyball uniform. Maybe I can wear it and not have to play. After all, Alice wears tracksuits all the time and never leaves the house.

Before I could close my door, Alice returned. "I almost forgot this," she said, handing me a schedule for the R.R.G.S.V.L., aka the Rancho Rosetta Girls' Summer Volleybarf League.

Here's the bad news:

Monday afternoon — volleyball.

Wednesday afternoon — volleyball.

Friday afternoon — volleyball.

And let's not forget SATURDAY mornings — volleyball.

It starts tomorrow.

Whoopie.

Love,

Emily

JUNE 22

Dear Dad,

Today was the first day of volleyball, and it was awful. The gym looked just like the one at Wilcox Academy, only a thousand times bigger. But instead of everyone I knew being there, it was full of everyone I didn't know. Still, I put on my best smile and tried to work the room.

The girl standing nearest to me was super tall, tan, skinny, and blond. Not blond like me, since my hair is darkish blond. Her blond was like sunshine-wheat-fields-gold-could-have-her-own-magazine blond. Plus, her teeth were really white and totally straight. She was so beautiful I couldn't help but stare.

"Hi, I'm Emily!"

The girl looked me over, and even though we were wearing the same uniform, I felt like I was dressed all wrong.

"I'm Julie," she answered.

"Have you played much volleyball before?" I asked. "It's such a violent sport, you know, spiking and hitting, ha-ha. . . ."

"Alyssa, Ariel, Ariana, and I have played together for years," she said.

I glanced at Alyssa, Ariel, and Ariana. They all looked the same, which was really weird since one of them was black, one was white, and one I'm not sure of. If Julie were a pop star, they'd be her backup singers.

"Volleyball is, like, our thing," Julie continued. "We even play for Rancho Rosetta Middle School."

"Hey, that's where I'll be going! I'm new. I was hoping to meet some kids before school starts, so it's great that we'll be on the same team this —"

"That's nice." Julie turned her back to me. I had no idea backs could be so expressive.

Some of the girls on the volleyball team are totally heartless, just like your song "Heartless Empty-Hearted Heartbreaker." There was this one Asian girl — you could just tell she didn't want to be there. She was all tense the entire time, though she did try to joke and pretend to know the height of the net and stuff like that. Then when we were practicing, the ball hit the girl on the head. I thought she was going to cry, especially when Julie and her backup singers started laughing. I should have gone up to the girl and asked if she was okay. If it happens again, I will. But I doubt she'll be back. She disappeared the minute practice was over, not even sticking around to help name the team.

"Serve-ivors?"

"I think that's a great name," Ariel or Alyssa or Ariana said.

"Thanks," said Julie. "It's so 'now.' Shall we vote?"

I miss Nicole and A.J. soooooo much. Funny, but when I was at Wilcox Academy I thought it was horrible that the school was so small, and that there were only twenty-five kids in my entire grade. Now I would give anything to be back.

"How was volleyball?" Alice asked when I got home. She's always grilling me.

"Horrible."

"It can't be that bad."

"Well, it is."

"You just need to give it a try."

"And you just need to give it a rest."

"Emily!"

I didn't wait to hear what she had to say. Later, when Alice was picking up dinner, I happened to be in her office. I found a partially eaten chocolate bar and bit off a piece. On the floor near her filing cabinets was a pile of books about divorce and how it affects kids. It affects kids in a bad way, okay? Does she need a book to figure that out?

I finished the chocolate bar, then gathered up all her divorce books and threw them in the neighbors' garbage can.

I hate Rancho Rosetta.

Love,

Emily

JUNE 24

Dear Dad,

I'm not sure what to do. Alice is in the bathroom crying. She's so loud it sounds fake, but I don't think it is.

She thinks I'm at the mall right now. I was headed there, but had to turn around to get my credit card.

Should I go in and ask her if she's okay? My stomach is in knots. I wish there was another grown-up around. What should I do?

Maybe I should just pretend I never heard her. Yes, that's what I'll do. It might embarrass her if she knew that I knew she cried like that. I don't feel like shopping now, but I need to get out of here fast.

Emily

JUNE 25

Dear Daddy,

Hooray! Hooray! Thanks for the postcard, I love it! The La Razel Luxury Spa and Resort. Is that where you're staying right now? It looks really ooh-la-la! I guess they have pretty fancy places in New Haven. I'm going to mark it on my map with a sticker.

Well, I've BeDazzled practically everything I own. You know what a BeDazzler is, right? It's that machine where you can put metal studs or jewels and stuff on clothing. I was going to BeDazzle your Members Only jacket, but I want to keep that in pristine condition since it may be in the Rock and Roll Hall of Fame someday. I considered BeDazzling TB, but decided against it. TB is not a flashy sort of teddy bear, although Miss Lucy Lion would look *fabulous* covered with gems.

I only have $1.34 left on my phone card. We've arranged it so when I call Nicole and A.J., they are on Nicole's dad's speakerphone. This might sound funny, but sometimes I dread talking to them. That's because one of them will just say something like "funnel cake" and the other will burst out laughing. I feel so lame because I have no idea what they are talking about. And when they tell me about going bowling or their latest sleepover, I just want to hang up. We used to be three best friends, but now it's like the two of them together and me way out here alone. I should be happy that they sound so happy, but I'm not. Am I a bad person?

Nicole and A.J. are leaving for camp soon. I still don't understand why I couldn't go with them. But Alice insisted I "get used to Rancho Rosetta before school starts." Get used to what? Being forced to play volleyball? Being ignored by the popular girls? Being away from you? Being a loner, probably for the rest of my life? And if that's not bad enough, I keep wandering around town and getting lost. Do you have any idea how humiliating it is to have to ask a stranger how to get home?

I hung around the mall again today. A lot of the salespeople know me. I kept seeing friends together. Big groups. Small groups. I saw three girls laughing as they ate ice cream. I wonder if they know how lucky they are.

They're probably spending the whole summer hanging out together, goofing off, and not playing volleyball.

Alice refused to listen to me when I told her I was never going back to the gym again. She said, "You should try to stick with something."

Okaaay, like how about sticking with marriage, Alice?

After the mall, I went to Stout's. Libby brought me a big slice of chocolate cake and I didn't even have to ask. Libby's cool, and not just because she has a butterfly tattoo. She's really easy to talk to. But, no offense to her, Libby's really old. Maybe fifty-ish. I wish I had at least one friend my own age here.

Love,
Emily

P.S. I love that you're using my address labels. Thanks again for the postcard. For a while I was scared you had forgotten about me. How silly is that???!!!

JUNE 26

Dear Dad,

Get this. I was lying on the couch with my feet over the back and my head hanging upside down, and suddenly

Alice squats down. She gets right in my face and says out of nowhere, "Emily, try to cheer up."

Right. Alice cries every afternoon at 2 p.m., and then has the nerve to tell me to be happier?! Uh, sure thing. You go first, Alice.

Actually, there is one thing to be happy about, but I'm going to try not to be too happy in case it doesn't work out. Remember that girl I told you about, the one who got hit on the head with a volleyball? Well, she did end up coming back to practice, and so did I. So anyway, today the volleyball was barreling its way toward this girl like some sort of missile, and do you know what she did? She squeezed her eyes shut, and then she *kicked* the ball.

Everyone on both sides of the net burst out laughing. Even Coach Gowin was in hysterics, though she tried to hide it. Yet the most amazing thing was that the girl just stood there with her head held high. She was so brave to stay put and take it. When I saw that, I just knew I had to meet her.

After the game (which we lost), I noticed her sitting alone in the gym. While most of us carried boring gym bags, hers looked exactly like a briefcase. That is so fashion-forward — a faux briefcase! I'll bet she reads Italian *Vogue*.

"Hi!" I said.

"How do you do?" she answered.

"I'm Emily and I just moved here. Don't you hate volleyball? Isn't Coach Gowin just awful? She reminds me of a potato with toothpick legs. Wouldn't you just love to get your hands on whoever gave her that whistle?"

She gave me a funny look, and I thought, *Oh no, I'm talking too much*. It's just that I haven't had anyone to talk to for weeks, other than Libby, and Alice doesn't count. But all of a sudden the girl says, "I'm Millicent L. Min. Yes. Yes. Ha! Yes."

How funny is that?

"What do you think of these outfits they force us to wear?" I asked.

Millicent looked down at her navy blue shorts and powder blue shirt. "It's nice," she said, "if you're fond of prison garb."

It was so fun talking to her. Millicent has a wonderfully deadpan sense of humor. Half the time you can't even tell if she's joking. Just as I was describing the hideous uniforms we had to wear at Wilcox Academy, Julie and her backup singers walked toward us. "Keep *her* away from the doughnuts," one of them said as she looked straight at me.

They all laughed, even though nothing was funny.

"That's a good one," I said, forcing a smile. "Thanks for the advice, but actually, I only eat healthy food!"

After they left, I tried to change the subject really fast. "My mom thinks volleyball will be good for me," I told Millicent. "You know, get coordinated and meet new people, blah, blah, blah." I offered her part of my Snickers bar.

"I thought you only ate healthy food," she said. She nibbled all the chocolate off the outside before popping the rest into her mouth.

"I just said that to make her feel bad," I confessed. "I know my dress size is in double digits, but Dr. Seto said I'm healthy, so what's the big deal? Now, tell me, why are you here? No offense, but you didn't look like you enjoyed yourself at all. In fact, a couple of times I was afraid you were going to cry."

Millicent sighed, and I hoped I hadn't hurt her feelings. "I don't have gym, I'm homeschooled." I looked at her carefully. I had never met anyone who was homeschooled before. "My parents want me to get more exercise," she continued, "even though I'm not really into sports."

"Me too! Plus I'm totally uncoordinated, and I don't like the idea of letting my teammates down."

Right on schedule, Julie returned.

"I hope you two won't hold the team back this year," she said in a sweet voice that was as insincere as her smile. "Most of us played together last year and we almost won first place."

"We're going to try our best," I said, shooting a smile at her. I felt braver now that I had a friend sitting next to me. "Right, Millie?"

I guess Millicent wasn't expecting my nudge, because she almost fell over. "Uh, right," she said.

"Good," Julie said. I loved how her smile fell off her face. "We all really want to win, that's all."

"We want to win too," I assured her. "We'll try hard, if you promise to try hard too."

"Uh . . . yeah, sure." Julie looked confused. "I promise."

Millie was quiet and I hoped I hadn't embarrassed her. I looked down, and there was this orange stuff on the floor all around her.

"Hey, do you mind if I ask you a personal question?"

She turned pale. "What is it?"

"Why are you sitting on your Cheetos?"

Millicent laughed. "I don't know, sometimes I just do weird things!"

"Me too! I'm glad you're not wearing white shorts."

"That would have been a disaster! I just thought maybe you were a health-food addict and would be opposed to Cheetos."

"Are you kidding? I love those, although Doritos are my favorite."

"What about Moon Pies?" Millie asked. "Do you like Moon Pies?"

"What's a Moon Pie?"

"'What's a Moon Pie?'" she squawked. "Oh Emily, you really have to try one."

"But what is it? Is it like a pie made of cheese?"

Millie laughed again. "Nooooo, it's, it's . . . round and made of graham cracker–like cookies and marshmallow dipped in chocolate."

"Ooooh, sounds great! Hey, wanna go get some ice cream? Or we could hang out at my house. My dad just bought me a new BeDazzler."

Millicent frowned and said, "Sorry, not today."

Ouch! I should have taken things more slowly and not just assumed we'd be friends. I was about to tell her I understood when she said, "How about some other time?"

"Really? I'd love to!"

"Me too!" Millie said, grinning.

She gave me her phone number and I already have it memorized. Happy, happy, happy! Maybe this summer won't be a total loss after all.

Love,
Emily

JUNE 29

Dear Daddy,

Alice was being a pain. Again.

"Please, please, please let me have a sleepover!!!" I had been thinking about this ever since I met Millicent. A.J., Nicole, and I had such fun at sleepovers.

"I didn't know you and this Millicent girl were such close friends."

"Well, we're not. Not yet, anyway. But I can just tell we will be. I have a good feeling about her. So can I ask her about a sleepover?"

"Emily, the house is a mess. Give it a week or two. I haven't even unpacked the plates."

"I can't wait two weeks. Two weeks is forever! You told me to go out and meet new people, and now that I finally met someone, you're saying I can't invite her over?"

Alice pulled something out of a box. It was her bat mitzvah photo. It's hard to believe she was ever my age.

"What do Millicent's parents do?"

"How should I know what they do?"

"Don't get defensive, I'm just curious."

"Alice, it's not like we sit around and discuss our parents' careers."

"Oh. I suppose not."

Alice was quiet as she set a picture of her mother on the mantel. She sighed. "I just wouldn't want your friend to think we live like this."

"But we do live like this," I reminded her as I gestured around the room. There were unopened boxes everywhere, and where there weren't boxes, there were massive piles of things, including a whole stack of Tupperware lids. Our house looked like a dump truck backed up and spilled everything out.

It was the opposite of our Allendale house, where everything was so orderly. It was as if we crossed some invisible line while we were driving across the country, where uptight, together Alice disappeared and scattered Alice took over. I thought of that movie you took me to, the one where space invaders inhabited human bodies. Is that what was happening to Alice? An alien takeover? It would explain a lot of things.

But what if Alice was right? What if Millicent Min came over and thought I lived like a total slob? What if she told all her friends, "We ate off of paper plates at Emily Ebers's house because they can't find their real plates"?

"I can clean it up," I said weakly.

Alice placed one of her diplomas next to my baby picture. I stiffened as she put her arm around me. "We can clean it up," she said. "Together. Then you can have your sleepover, okay?"

What choice did I have?

"Okay."

The rest of the day was a miracle. Maybe you heard about it on the news: Alice's computer remained off! By evening we were exhausted, and when we stopped to admire our progress, we were shocked. Now there were empty boxes scattered on one side of the house and piles of junk on the other.

"The house looks worse than when we started!" I moaned.

"Don't worry," Alice said. "We'll take it one room at a time, starting with your room. But first, food."

Ah yes, dinner. That meant one of two things: frozen

food or Stout's. I wonder if there's something about divorce that makes people stop cooking? Alice never makes those lavish meals anymore. And you, you never had any food in your apartment. Remember when I was little and you used to make pancakes on Sunday mornings? I miss that. I found your favorite frying pan in one of the boxes. I put it under my bed for safekeeping.

Don't take this the wrong way, but your apartment sort of depresses me. Probably because there's hardly anything in it, although all your speakers are awesome. I know — maybe you can get on that *Compartment Apartment* show where they redo your place while you're out. And when the television cameras surprise you, you could tell them about the Talky Boys and maybe even play a song, and tell them about how famous you used to be!

I'm going to ask Libby if she can add "Heartless Empty-Hearted Heartbreaker" to the jukebox at Stout's. We ate there again tonight.

"You two ladies been busy?" Libby asked.

"I'm doing the final edits on an article called 'What Happened to All of the Hippies?'" Alice replied.

Libby's eyes lit up. "You're looking at one of the original hippies right here!"

"Really?" Alice said, sitting up straighter. "Could we talk about this tomorrow morning? The article isn't due till the afternoon."

"Right on," said Libby, giving us the peace sign.

As we ate dinner, Alice said, "I think I knew Libby

was a hippie. She's about the right age, and there's something carefree and open about her."

We both looked at Libby, who was chatting with a policeman and laughing.

After dinner Libby announced, "Tonight we have jumbleberry pie, and there's lemon meringue made from lemons from my yard, and, Emily, there's French silk."

"French silk, Emily!" Alice said, giving Libby a smile.

French silk is my favorite pie. I'm not really one for cooked fruit, but I *love* piecrust. That's why you and I were so good together. You loved the fruit and hated crust. I loved the crust and hated the fruit.

"French silk . . ." Libby sang.

Just the thought of chocolate and crust was almost enough to make me dizzy. But I heard myself telling Libby, "We're sort of in a hurry tonight."

"Tell you what," Alice jumped in. "Give us a slice of French silk to go."

By the time we got back home, I was ready to tackle my room. As Mongo Bongo kept us energized, we worked like the high-speed version of Maggie and Lola from *Compartment Apartment.* We were having trouble getting the posters of *The Surfers of Solana Beach* straight, so Alice suggested we just put everything on angles. (I guess she does have some good ideas now and then.) I even put up that old poster of the Talky Boys, the one where you had big hair and are sitting on a motorcycle.

Finally, Alice handed me the hammer and climbed

down the ladder. I yanked on the pull chain, and suddenly my room was bathed with soft blue light from the Japanese paper lantern you bought me with my credit card. It turned the purple walls lavender.

"I think your friend will be most impressed," Alice murmured. "Does she like purple?"

I nodded, even though I didn't know.

"Okay, Emily, off to bed for you, and back to work for me."

"It's after midnight," I squawked. "You're going to work after all this?"

"I've still got to finish up my hippie article. It's due tomorrow."

"But you spent all day working on my room. . . ."

"It's okay, I'm actually reenergized just thinking about the article. I envy the outlook hippies had on life. They didn't let stress get to them. Have you noticed how easygoing Libby is?" I nodded. "Good night, Emily." She looked tired but content.

"Good night, Alice."

From my room I could hear her computer turn on. I ran to her office.

"Emily?"

"Thank you."

The glow from her screen bathed the room in blue, like the light from my Japanese lantern. "Anytime, honey," she said.

I'm going to get ready for bed now. I'm pretty tired.

Do you ever have trouble sleeping? Sometimes I do. I've never seen Alice sleep, but I know she has to because she says she has bad dreams.

Oh! I almost forgot to tell you, I put pink heart stickers all over my walls. You can see them when you visit. Until then, here's one of your very own. . . .

ZZZzzzzz,
Emily

JUNE 30

Hi Daddy!
Millicent Min and I are sooooooo much alike that we're practically twins. Except that she is Chinese, about five inches shorter than me, and fifty pounds lighter. Oh, and she has bangs and shoulder-length straight black hair and dark brown eyes, and I have thick brownish-blond hair and light brown eyes. But Millie and I get along so well. When we talk it feels like I've known her forever. Have you ever felt that way about someone?

I called her today about the sleepover.

"Hi Millie, it's me!"

"Me who?" she asked, using a really funny fake formal voice.

"Me, Emily Ebers. Wanna come over to my house for a sleepover on Tuesday?"

There was total silence. Alice says that if you don't recharge the batteries on cordless phones, they can go dead. "Hello? Hello, Millie, are you there? Millie, are you still there? Hellooooo . . . ?"

"I'm still here," I finally heard her say.

"I'm afraid we might have a bad connection."

"No, no, the connection's just fine."

"Okay then, as I was saying, if you don't want to come to my house, maybe I can come to yours."

"I don't think that's a good idea. . . ."

For a moment I was scared that she didn't want to have a sleepover and I would never make any friends in Rancho Rosetta. But when she didn't say anything else, I jumped in and said really fast, "Then it's settled, you'll come here!"

"Emily, I'd like to speak to Millicent's mother," Alice interrupted. I didn't even see her come into the room.

I covered the phone. "Why?" I cringed.

"Hello?" I could hear Millie calling. "Hello?"

"Emily." Alice gave me her do-what-I-tell-you-to-do-or-else-you-are-in-so-much-trouble look.

"Millie, my mom wants to talk to your mom."

"Oh."

"Exactly."

Alice took the phone. "Hello! This is Alice Ebers speaking. . . . Yes, well, yes, we would love to have Millicent stay over. . . . She can? Wonderful, Emily really could use a friend. She's been out of sorts ever since we left New Jersey. . . ."

Urgggg, leave it to Alice to totally humiliate me. What other embarrassing things was she going to tell Mrs. Min? Or what if Alice decided to have one of her mood swings and suddenly started sobbing?

I snuck out.

At the grocery store I stocked up on popcorn and Snickers bars, since I know Millie likes those. (I put the Snickers in the mini-fridge in my room so they'll be nice and cold.) I also got some magazines, strawberry air freshener, and Triple Badoobadoo Bubble Gum.

Someone had stacked Brillo Pads into a pyramid that almost reached the ceiling. I resisted the urge to knock it over, but it was hard. Then right when I was about to get some Cheetos, I gasped. The best-looking boy in the entire world was headed toward me.

Ohmygosh, he was totally to die for! He looked like a really tall movie star, only better. His hair was shaved close to his head, but I think it was light brown. His eyes were greenish-gray, he was wearing a basketball shirt and shorts, and he had the lean muscles of a total jock. I couldn't help gawking at him. Before I knew what was happening, I heard myself saying, "Do you like Cheetos? I love Cheetos, they are so crunchy and yummy."

Crunchy and yummy?

He looked at me like I was a scary person, but my mouth kept going. "The thing about Cheetos is that their bags are always puffy. Have you noticed that? I used to think they were trying to cheat us, but really it's so the Cheetos don't get smashed. I saw that on the Food Network. Do you like TV? I hate it when all that's left in the bottom of the chip bags are little pieces, don't you?"

The boy blinked a few times, then reached for the Doritos.

"Oh! Doritos. I love those too. Can you get a bag for me, please? They are so tall. I mean, you are so tall. I mean, I can't reach because I am so tall. . . ."

He handed me the bag, got one for himself, then strolled away in silence.

Oooooh, on a scale of one to ten, I would have rated him a 100! I can't wait to tell Millicent about him.

I grabbed the Cheetos and ran to the checkout line, almost crashing into the Brillo pyramid. Sadly, I was too late. He was gone. This girl Wendy from volleyball was standing near the shopping carts with her mouth hanging open. When she saw me, we grinned at each other, both appreciating what we had just seen.

If this is what the boys in Rancho Rosetta look like, then I think I'm going to like it here after all.

When I got home, Alice chided me. "Emily, next time you leave the house, at least leave me a note so I know where you are."

"The sleepover is on, right?" I asked.

"It's on. Oh, and there's some mail for you," Alice said, gesturing to the kitchen table.

It was your postcard from Boston. Hoorah! The Hotel Stambler looks really nice and classy. I can't believe you had a butler on your floor! It sounds like you're having a lot of fun. I'm finally starting to have some fun too.

Love,
Emily!!!

JULY 2

Dear Dad,

I was so happy this afternoon because today was the day my very first friend from Rancho Rosetta was coming to sleep over. Then I walked into the kitchen and it was as if I stepped into a horror movie.

"What are you wearing??!!!" I screamed.

Alice twirled around. She was wearing a long patch-work skirt, a tie-dyed top, a floppy hat, and ugly sandals. "Do you like it?"

"Where did you get that? Don't tell me they sell those kinds of clothes in Rancho Rosetta!"

"The hat was a gift from Libby, and the rest was from eBay, where else?"

Of course. Alice does everything by computer. It's her best and only friend. I just wish her friend would tell her how dumb she looks.

"I think it looks good," Alice said defensively. "It's vintage."

"'Vintage' just means used," I muttered.

She ignored me. "I admire the hippies and their relaxed attitude toward life. Unhampered by rules and regulations, the flower children were able to love and be loved freely. Look!" she said, holding out her hand. "It's a mood ring."

"It's black."

"Well, yes, I'm a little tense right now."

"Not as tense as I am." I have a guest coming over and my mother is dressed for Halloween. This is worse than the time you told her you really liked curly hair, and she went out and got that perm that made her head look like a big fuzz ball.

I headed outside to wait for Millicent, but to my surprise she was just getting out of her mom's car. I ran up to her. "Oh, Millie!" I cried. "I'm so excited! You're my very first guest!"

A barefoot Alice headed toward Mrs. Min. Before she could embarrass me any further, I rushed Millie into the house.

She came inside, stopped, and stared at the piles of books still on the floor. Then she looked at Alice's awards on the fireplace mantel.

"Millicent, your mother is so nice," Alice said a few minutes later as she shut the door. Millie was still gawking. "Oh! Please forgive me for all the books. I just haven't gotten around to organizing yet."

I worried that Millie would bolt, but instead she exclaimed, "You're Alice X. Ebers, the journalist?"

Millicent Min had heard of my mother? How weird was that?

"Yes, I'm that Alice X. Ebers." She looked pleased with herself. "Although around here I'm just plain Alice. You know of my work?"

"My mom mentioned that you wrote," she said. "What are you working on now?" Millie was really good at faking interest in Alice. *Good strategy*, I thought. *Get her on your side.*

"Well, I just finished up a feature called 'What Happened to All of the Hippies?' Tomorrow I start a new article tentatively titled 'The Bard of Brooklyn' and I'm also working on some investigative pieces, including one about young millionaires called 'Eight Enterprising Entrepreneurs.'"

Snooze alert! Snooze alert! Snooze alert!

"We gotta go!" I grabbed Millicent by the arm. "Come on, this way!"

As I gave her the tour, I pretended that I was you at an Open House.

"Twenty-eight-hundred square feet, two fireplaces, and four bedrooms, two with walk-in closets," I told Millie. "Here's a generously sized living room with fireplace number one, and a family room with the second fireplace. There are three bathrooms, a washer and dryer, plus all-new stainless-steel appliances in the kitchen and a sprinkler system in the backyard."

"This place is huge!" Millie said.

"Yeah. It's a lot bigger than our old house, but I like that one better," I admitted, "even though it was falling apart."

"We live in a mail-order house from Sears," Millie said. "It's really small and decrepit. My mother keeps saying, 'It has character,' which means, 'We can't afford anything else right now.'"

"Wow, you can get houses from department stores? I've always thought it would be cool to live in a department store, or better yet, a mall!"

"I've read about a mall that has condos in it."

"No way!"

When Alice called out, "Girls, time for dinner!" I couldn't believe three hours had flown by. It was so much fun talking to Millicent Min. Alice thought so too. Millie sat across from her and kept asking questions, then actually listening to the answers! I can tell she's one of those kids who's good with grown-ups.

"It's fascinating that you're a journalist," Millie said as she reached for the pepper. Alice had made microwave dinners, her new specialty. I warned her ahead of time that Millicent was a vegetarian, so she nuked some mushroom thing for her.

"Well, I really love my job. I'm lucky. Not a lot of people can say that."

"What do you like about it?" Millie asked, putting a sincere look on her face.

"Excellent question! Let me think." Alice set down her fork and smiled at Millicent. "The truth," she finally answered. "My mentor at Columbia, John Vandercook, used to say, 'A journalist's mission is to uncover the truth and then tell it, even if it's not what people want to hear.' Sometimes I write about popular culture, other times about unpopular topics no one really wants to consider. But through it all, I always strive to reveal the truth."

"Wow," Millicent said without cracking up. "That's so cool."

Alice mistook her sarcasm for interest and beamed. I hadn't seen her this happy since . . . since . . . well, I can't even remember when. Then, unprompted, she dished out a long and totally mind-numbing history of her journalism career. Finally, Millie tried to change the subject by asking, "What brought you to Rancho Rosetta?"

"I wrote an article on the top one hundred places to raise children," Alice said, glancing my way. "Rancho Rosetta was in the top twenty-five, and I just fell in love with it. I love research, it makes life so much more orderly."

I tried not to snicker. This statement was coming from a woman dressed in clashing patterns and wearing a silly hat.

"I agree." Millie nodded. "It must be so neat to have you for a mom."

"Oh, I don't know about that." Alice smiled at me. "Is it neat to have me as a mom?"

Nothing like being put on the spot. What was I supposed to say? That it's neat to be uprooted from all your friends and the only life you've ever known? That it's neat to have a mom who divorces your dad and drags you clear across the country? That it's neat never knowing if she's going to be crying or laughing?

Both Millie and Alice were waiting for my answer.

"I dunno," I said. "You're my mom, just a regular mom."

Alice's smile wavered slightly before she jumped up and ran out of the room. Millie looked puzzled. I shrugged and took another bite of chicken.

A moment later, Alice returned.

"I thought you girls might like this. I just bought it this afternoon in your honor, Millicent."

"Not again," I moaned as I waved away the smoke. "Alice, you know I hate that stuff."

(Sorry, Dad. I know you love incense, but I still can't stand it.)

I tried not to gag. Millie tried not to cough. Alice and I engaged in a stare-down through the haze.

Finally, Millicent made a joke to break the tension. "In my family we do not smoke marijuana, not even for medicinal purposes."

"Nor do we," Alice said. "It's against the law, you know. However, I hope you have no objection to sandal-wood incense."

"That's not marijuana?" Millie said.

"Emily!" Alice said as she burst out laughing. "Your friend is so funny. What a great sense of humor!"

At last, dinner ended. Before Alice could bore us with more facts about hippies and "their resolve to lead happier, more carefree lives, predicated on peace and love," I resolved to rescue Millie, and we made a hasty retreat to my room.

"These are my stuffed animals," I said proudly. She looked impressed with my collection. "You stand still," I directed, "while I make Shamu swim around you, okay? Shamu loves to swim around rocky shores."

"Is this considered normal?" Millicent asked. She was seriously good at standing still. "I mean, is this a regular sleepover activity?"

"Sorry," I laughed. "Borrr-ing! Let's do something else. Do you like beads? Everyone likes beads. I love beads! Oh yes, let's bead."

I brought out my new plastic bead kit, the one you bought me last week with the "forty-two new and exciting designs!!!" I made my necklace really fast, but Millie took forever.

"Wow!" I exclaimed when she finally held up her masterpiece. Millicent had made a pattern using different colors, animal beads, and a peace symbol. You could tell she had done this before. My necklace was just random colors in random order.

"It's beautiful!" I told Millie. "Oh! I know! We should exchange necklaces as a sign of good luck and friendship." When she hesitated, I quickly added, "Unless you don't want to. I mean, yours is so pretty, and mine's just colors."

Millicent looked at her necklace. "It's just that I made this . . . and . . . and . . . why not? Yes! Let's exchange them."

I couldn't wait to put on the necklace Millie made. It was like the exchange sealed our friendship. I've never even done that with Nicole or A.J., although once we all bought the same bracelet except in different colors with different charms on them.

Just as we were trying to figure out what to do next, Alice called us into the living room. She had made popcorn and sprinkled Tabasco sauce on it, the way you like it. We were about to take the popcorn into my room when I heard the words that sent chills down my spine.

"Hey, ladies, this song is for the magnificent Millicent Min. . . ."

I turned around and released a silent scream as Alice brought the microphone up to her mouth. Dad, why didn't you take your karaoke machine with you? With every bad note Alice hit, I died a thousand deaths. And she hit a lot of bad notes.

"Come on, Millie, sing along," Alice shouted over the music.

Millicent rose cautiously.

"You don't have to do it," I yelled. I don't think she heard me.

I watched in horror as Alice forced Millie to sing. They started with the Rolling Stones' song "Jumpin' Jack Flash," and every time they got to the word "jumpin'," Alice would jump. When it became clear that Millicent really didn't know any of the words, that didn't stop Alice. Out of nowhere she produced her *K-K-KRAZY FOR KARAOKE* book of lyrics. Millicent pored over it and settled on "Strawberry Fields Forever" by the Beatles. "Oh!" Alice said. "Very 1960s. Very hippie-ish!"

As she sang, and Alice danced in her geeky, jerky way, I wondered if Millicent would ever want to come to my house again.

Before we went to sleep I told her, "I am soooooo sorry."

"Whatever for?" Millie had chosen the bottom bunk.

"My mom is so weird. I can't believe she forced you to sing with her. And I hate incense. It makes me ill. I think she goes out of her way to embarrass me."

"Really? I thought she was cool."

"You do?" I was soooo relieved.

"Truly."

"Oh Millie, you're the one who's too cool!"

I guess good can come out of volleyball.

Love,

Emily

JULY 3

Dear Dad,

As soon as Millie got home I called her.

"Hi Millicent, it's me!"

"Me who?"

"You weirdo, it's me, Emily!"

"I thought it was you!"

"Hey, I just wanted to tell you that you're the first person I'm putting on my speed dial."

"Really? Wow! Okay, I'm going to put you on our speed dial too."

"Okay, good-bye!"

"Bye, Emily, talk to you later!"

The instant I hung up the phone, it rang.

"Hello?"

"Hi, it's me, Millicent L. Min, from volleyball."

"Millie?"

"Just checking to see if the speed dial works. Okay, good-bye!"

Isn't she just the funniest person you've ever heard of? Just thinking about Millie makes me smile.

Love,

Emily

JULY 4

Dear Dad,

Tonight was the big fireworks show. I called Millie and invited her to go with us but she had to do something with her parents. I hope she's not getting tired of me. Sometimes she acts a little strange, like she's holding back, and it makes me wonder if I'm being too forward.

"Alice, if we're going to see the fireworks, we have to leave soon."

"In a minute, in a minute," she kept saying, like it was some sort of chant. One hour (that would be sixty "in-a-minutes") later we left the house. The park was pretty crowded, but no one seemed to mind. Some people brought lawn chairs. Lots were wearing Uncle Sam hats. I was glad I had BeDazzled my T-shirt with red and blue gems. Alice wore cutoff jeans and some sort of flowy flowery gauze top. I prayed that it would get dark soon and no one would see me with her.

A boy with a huge mass of curly dark hair walked past us selling sparklers. Alice said he was an enterprising entrepreneur and wanted to talk to him, but I stopped her before she could hassle him.

Just then the speakers crackled and everyone sang "The Star-Spangled Banner." I could not believe how loud Alice was. Why does she even bother to sing? You're the singer in the family.

Remember that Fourth of July at the beach when I was little? There was a full moon and we stretched a blanket across the sand. Alice got cold, so you hugged her to warm her up. Then I snuggled between both of you and we watched the fireworks together.

Tonight I imagined that wherever you were, you were looking up in the sky too. And even though we might not have seen the same fireworks, at least we were admiring the same moon.

Love,
Emily

JULY 5

Dear Dad,
Millie is determined to be my personal Rancho Rosetta tour guide. Today after volleyball she announced, "This afternoon's field trip will be to the Rialto movie theater!"

I was happy to get away from volleyball. It's becoming pretty clear that I'm lousy at it. Coach Gowin and Julie keep shaking their heads when I mess up. The only person worse than me is Millie, though I would never tell her that. She doesn't seem to notice how bad she is. When people make fun of her, it's like she can't hear them. One time, though, Millicent almost got the ball over the net, and Wendy, the nice girl, complimented her on it. I know Millie heard that because she couldn't stop smiling.

"What movies are playing?" I asked as we walked out of the gym into the sunlight. It was so bright I was almost blinded.

"Just one," she said. "It's a Marx Brothers classic called *A Day at the Races*."

Can you believe it? A movie theater that shows only one movie!

The Rialto looked really old and run-down on the outside, but the inside was incredible.

"Where's Maddie?" the ticket seller asked.

"She's got her yoga class," Millie explained. "This is my friend Emily."

As we headed into the theater, the ticket seller raced past us and stood at the door. We handed her our tickets and she tore them in half, then beat us to the concession stand.

"What can I get for you?"

"The regular, times two," Millie told her.

"Millie, shall I just put this on your tab?" she asked as she handed over popcorn and sodas.

"Yes, please."

How cool is that?

The theater was practically empty, so we sat right in the very middle. I looked up. There was a mural of angels on the ceiling. Suddenly, the red velvet drapes parted, and I was so startled that I almost forgot how lumpy the seats felt.

There were no previews. The movie just began. "Something's wrong," I whispered to Millie. "It's in black and white."

Without taking her eyes off the screen, she answered, "A lot of the classics are in black and white, but once you get into them it doesn't matter what color they are."

Millicent was right. The movie was great, and we laughed all the way through it. You would have had a blast.

Afterward, even though we were full of popcorn, Millie took me to this hot-dog stand called Mel's that's in the shape of a mustard jar. For a skinny person, Millicent really eats a lot. She says she has a high metabolism.

"I'd like a high metabolism," I said as I bit into a chili-cheese dog. It was soooo good. "Where can I get one?"

"Oh, you have to be born with it," she said between bites of cheese fries.

"I know. Joking!"

"I was just joking too," Millie said, wiping her hands. "Come on, Emily. I want to show you someplace special."

We threw away our trash and headed out. It was hard keeping up with Millicent. She walks really fast, like she's always late, only she never is.

"Where are you taking me?"

We passed over a bridge and headed toward the train tracks. It was a part of town I had never seen before.

"You'll see. We're almost there. Don't worry, it will be worth it."

Big stinky trucks kept rumbling past us, but they didn't seem to bother Millie.

"Here we are!" she finally said, looking pleased.

"What is this place?" I held my nose.

"The recycling plant. Isn't it magnificent? Garbage goes in and recyclable material comes out."

I don't know anyone at Wilcox Academy who would consider a recycling plant magnificent.

"The Earth thanks you!" Millicent shouted as the trucks rolled past. "We thank you! Reclaim, recycle, reuse!"

Even though I was surrounded by stink and garbage, I caught Millie's enthusiasm. "The Earth thanks you! We thank you!" I shouted. "Great job!"

Some of the drivers honked their horns and waved. One woman called out, "Hi Millicent!"

Millie and I grinned at each other as we cheered on the drivers. Hanging around with her is such an adventure.

As we walked back to my house, I said, "I've had so much fun! Maybe tomorrow you can show me around school."

Millie slowed down and grew quiet. "I don't go to the middle school," she mumbled.

"Oh! Sorry, my fault. I forgot you're homeschooled. Never mind, it's no big deal."

Millicent didn't talk much the rest of the way home.

Obviously, school was a painful subject for her. I felt terrible.

Love,
Emily

JULY 6

Dear Dad,

This morning at breakfast, Alice wanted to talk about you.

"Emily, I think it's time we discussed the divorce. We can't keep sidestepping the issue."

The yolk from my eggs over easy oozed out onto the plate and toward the toast. I did nothing to stop it.

"He left you and then came back," I said matter-of-factly. "Then you separated again, and got back together once more. Then you divorced him. After that you were still mad at him, so you moved us here to make it hard for me to see him ever again."

"Emily, that's not true. . . ."

"Yes, it is," I screamed. "I don't want to hear any of your excuses. I know what you want. You want me to say it's okay that you divorced Daddy. But you know what? It's not okay!"

"Emily . . ." she said weakly. Her mood ring was black.

I pushed my plate away and ran to my room. As I

sobbed, I could hear Alice crying in the hallway. More than anything else in the world I needed a hug, but I just could not bring myself to open the door.

Why can't the two of you just say you're sorry and get back together? What's so hard about that? People make mistakes all the time.

Listen, I'll make you a deal. Just talk to Alice, and I'll organize your sheet music. I'll wax your car. I'll do whatever you want. Just talk to her. If you do, I'll never ask you for anything ever again. I'll even give you the credit card back. Just talk to her and tell her everything's going to be okay. She is so sad.

Tonight, Libby could tell there was something seriously wrong. She brought a slice of French silk pie for me and a slice of apple pie and a cup of coffee for Alice all "on the house."

"Won't you get in trouble for giving this to us for free?" I asked.

Libby waved her hand in the air. "Naw, I never get in trouble around here. What's the worst thing that could happen? I could get fired?" She laughed as if she had just made a funny joke.

As I was poking at my pie, I saw Wendy's family sitting in a back booth. Her little brother kept trying to steal her French fries, and her parents just laughed at the two of them.

When we left, Wendy called out, "Bye, Emily! See you tomorrow!"

"Oh, is she on your volleyball team?" Alice asked.

"Maybe."

"How is volleyball going?"

"Fine."

"Do you like your coach?"

"Maybe."

"Emily, can we talk?"

"No."

See? See how hard it is with her around? Oh, Daddy, I know she's impossible, but won't you just try one more time to get along with her? Maybe you don't have to get married again. Maybe you could just date or be friends. Or at least not hate each other.

Love,

Emily

JULY 7

Hi Dad,

This morning, I bought a new sleeping bag with my credit card. But don't worry, it was on sale, and it was a necessity, because right now I'm on a sleepover at Millie's! Her parents are sooooo much fun! Get this, Millie's dad collects TOYS! He's got Matchbox cars, just like you, only tons more. He even has these old-fashioned plastic robots that box. We went three rounds before Millie made us stop.

We had the *best* dinner — veggie lasagna and a salad with avocados (the Mins have their *own* avocado tree), and homemade brownies! Millie says her family doesn't eat out too often because they are on a budget. I once heard Alice say that all the money you made when you were a rock star disappeared. Is that why you had to give up being a full-time musician and become a real estate agent, because of money?

When we first saw our new house, I asked Alice how much money she makes, but she refused to tell me. Why do adults get so weirded out about money? When I have kids, I'm going to tell them everything. I will hold nothing back. In fact, I'm going to be exactly like Millicent's mom. She treats us like grown-ups. And Millie's dad is more like a friend than a father.

Everything about the Mins is great. Millie even has her own tree house in the backyard. And her room is so unique. There's a *washer and dryer* in it! Plus she's totally nailed that stark look that's so big on that home-decorating show, *Less Is More with Leslie Moore*. Millicent Min is a total trendsetter. As she was telling me about her summer school class, I began poking around her room, and I saw something sticking out from under her bed. Millicent saw me and immediately pushed it back. Which, of course, made me really, really, really want to know what was in it. Candy? Diamonds? Love letters?

"What's in there, Millie?" I asked.

"Nothing."

"Oh, show me!" I pleaded.

"It's just old socks," she said.

I grabbed the box, hoping it was something wonderful, and it was. The box was filled with comics! Millie and I have *exactly* the same taste!! Betty & Veronica rule!!!

"Why can't Archie see that Veronica is evil?"

"I know!" Millie agreed. "Betty is so nice and she always gets overlooked. What's Archie's problem? It's clear that Betty belongs with him, and Veronica and Reggie should go together."

We were doing our nails and talking Archie when Mrs. Min came in with an empty laundry basket. She looks really young for a mom. Her skin is so smooth, and her hair is jet-black and shoulder-length and shiny, like Millicent's. I love the way Mrs. Min laughs. Millie's parents laugh a lot. They don't act like married people. They act like they are in love.

I offered to help fold towels, but Mrs. Min said, "That's all right, Emily. This is the last load. I'll leave you girls alone now. Oh! But when your nails dry, we've got a fresh box of Moon Pies."

Mille and I looked at each other and yelled, "Moon Pies!" They're my new favorite food. That, and frozen grapes. Millie introduced me to those too.

"You are so lucky," I told her after Mrs. Min shut the door. "Your parents are so normal."

Millie burst out laughing, like I had made the funniest joke in the world. Before long, I was laughing with her. Then we read Archie comics out loud until our sides hurt from giggling and we could barely breathe.

I imagine that being on the road with the Talky Boys is like one long sleepover. I hope you're having a wonderful time. I am.

Love,
Emily

JULY 8

Dear Dad,

I finally got a letter from A.J. and Nicole. They cowrote it. Every other sentence Nicole wrote in red and A.J. wrote in blue. They said they were having the best time ever at camp, and even won the "Most Likely to Be Twins Separated at Birth" contest. Enclosed was a photo of them wearing matching baby-blue shorts and red tank tops. Both had cut their hair in the same style. They looked like strangers to me.

Love,
Emily

JULY 9

Dear Dad,

Another postcard! I love it when I open the mailbox and there's one waiting for me, like a present. It seems like we're in touch more now than when we lived near each other. (Kidding!) Are you enjoying Concord? Isn't there a grape named after that city? I added a sticker on my map. I can see you are headed north.

The Sunset Suites seem like a nice place. It's cool that you get your own room. Do you jump on the bed? Remember when we did that on our Myrtle Beach vacation? The postcard says that they serve "a complimentary sunrise breakfast" and every room has a view. From my bedroom I can see our neighbor's backyard. Mrs. Neederman has three identical white doghouses all lined up in a neat row.

It sounds like your tour is still going great. I wish I could be there. This morning I listened to "The Emily Song" over and over while I decorated the cover to this letter journal. It's going to look so nice. I bought a bunch of stuff at the craft store, including metallic buttons, gold paint, and even a peacock feather. I can't wait until you get this. Won't you be surprised!

Love,

E

JULY 10

Dear Dad,

Today Millicent took me to her grandmother's house. At first I didn't want to go. Grandma Emmaline doesn't know I exist, and Grammy Ebers was always kind of, well, you know . . . not the most cheerful person in the world.

"Maddie's not like that," Millicent insisted. "She likes everyone, and it seems to be mutual."

I was so glad Millie forced me to go. Maddie — that's short for Madison — has colorful bowling balls in her garden and a major collection of snow globes ("One from every state, and several from Guam") in her house. Plus, there's a huge wooden dragon in the bathroom ("That's Julius, he's in time-out right now") and photos and paintings on every inch of wall ("No sense in wasting blank space").

Maddie doesn't act old at all. Even though she's sort of round, she can do the most amazing kung fu moves. She tried to teach some to Millie and me, but somehow the three of us ended up in a heap and we couldn't get up because we were laughing so hard.

"Do you like homemade chocolate-chip cookies, Emily?" Maddie asked when we finally got to our feet.

"Oh, I love them!"

"Me too," she said before she disappeared into the kitchen.

Millie lowered her voice. "You know, she can't bake

at all. She buys everything from the store or Butterfield's Bakery and pretends they are hers."

"Well, they are hers if she bought them," I noted.

"Good point."

"Ta-da!" Maddie reappeared with a tray of cookies and lemonade.

"These are delicious," I told her.

She lowered her eyes modestly and said, "Yes, I have to agree with you." I took another bite. "Say, Emily," Maddie said, her face lighting up. "How would you like your tea leaves read? I can predict the future, you know."

"You can? Really? Yes, yes, oh please read my tea leaves!"

As Maddie brewed tea, Millie and I wandered around the house. There were lots of photos of her grandfather everywhere. He was always smiling, like he was in on a funny joke. "This one looks like a mug shot," I observed.

"It is," Millicent said. "My dad's parents play bridge and golf for fun. My mom's parents go to jail."

Maddie called out from the kitchen, "Yes, but we weren't criminals, we were activists. There's a big difference!"

Millie rolled her eyes. Maddie started singing. Her voice was almost as bad as Alice's, only her singing didn't bother me. "Emmmmee-leeee, so pretty," and "Millieeeeee, loves her treeeee."

Millie and I looked at each other and tried not to giggle.

"Okay! Ready or not, here I come!" Maddie shouted.

There were three cups on the tray, one for each of us. Maddie read Millicent's tea leaves first. After staring at Millicent's cup for a long time, she waved her hands over it three times, then said in a low deep voice, "I see a long-sustaining friendship in your future. But the leaves are telling me, you must learn to trust yourself before you can trust the world around you."

Instead of thanking her, Millie made a face. Maddie didn't seem to notice.

"You next, Emily!"

I scooted my chair right up next to hers and held on to my friendship necklace for good luck. Maddie smelled like gingerbread. Slowly, she shook the cup so that the tea leaves swirled like couples waltzing around a dance floor. At last the leaves stopped. Most settled to the bottom. A few floated on top. Maddie peered into the cup. I did too, even though I wasn't sure what we were looking at.

"I see a happy girl who has had some troubles," she began. I gulped and stared harder at the tea leaves. "Wait, there's more," Maddie said, holding up her hand. She leaned toward me and whispered, "There's always more." My eyes widened. "Emily Ebers, a lot of changes are ahead, but try not to worry too much. Change is not always bad. You have embarked on a journey that will take you far, but it's up to you to decide where you are headed."

"Will it be a good journey?" I could feel my insides quiver. This was better than A.J.'s Ouija board.

"Ah, the leaves do not answer that."

"But how will I know where to go? What if I get lost? I always get lost."

"Maddie," Millicent interrupted. "Do you really believe this stuff? I thought you said that the Magic 8 Ball was the only true predictor of the future."

Her grandmother did not answer. Instead she was peering into the third cup of tea. "Ah!" Maddie exclaimed. "Just as I thought!"

As she closed her eyes and sipped her tea, I started to ask her what it was she saw. But by the way she was smiling, I could tell she was having a pleasant time enjoying her own secret.

Love,
Emily

JULY 11

Dear Dad,

This afternoon I met Millie at the drugstore. I needed more Bonne Bell Lip Smackers. I've lost three since we moved here.

"Oh! Let's buy makeup and do makeovers on each other," I exclaimed as we neared the cosmetics aisle.

"Oh! Okay," Millicent replied as she walked briskly

past the lipsticks. "But first let's poke ourselves in the eyes with a fork, since that would be so much more fun."

Later, when Millie and I were in line, it felt like someone was staring at me. I slowly turned around, and it was as if my body had been struck by a million billion jolts of electricity.

Standing in the very next line was this Asian boy with black hair, big beautiful brown eyes, and long eyelashes. I smiled at him, and he smiled back. His grin was crooked and totally to die for. Do you believe in love at first sight? (Do you still believe in love?)

The boy was staring at me staring at him. Just when it looked like he was going to say something, Millie whirled around. His eyes went from me to her, and instantly his smile disappeared.

"Millie, you're all red. Do you know him?" I whispered. "Is he from around here? Oh, he's soooo dreamy."

"Looks like a nightmare to me," she muttered. As we turned back to check him out again, he tossed something and ran. The alarm shrieked as he bolted out the emergency exit. I scooped up what he had dropped — a tube of Zappo Zit — and slipped it in with the things I was buying.

As we walked to Maddie's house, I had so many questions. "So, Millicent, do you know him? It looked like you knew each other. I wonder what he thought of me? Do you think he's thinking about me right now? I sensed a real connection, like they say you can get when you find your soul mate. I wonder if he's my soul mate? I mean, I really felt like we were speaking through our eyes. Do you think people can speak through their eyes? Don't you think he has the dreamiest eyes? And his smile, I could talk about his smile for . . ."

"ENOUGH!!!" Millicent yelled. "If I hear one more word about that stupid boy, I'm going to regurgitate my entire lunch and a good deal of my breakfast too!"

"Oh. Sorry."

I held on to my necklace and hoped that I would see him again — soon. I wonder what Millie has against him. I'll ask again later. In the meantime, I'm going to sleep with his Zappo Zit under my pillow.

Love,

Emily

JULY 13

Hi Daddy,

Loved the postcard from Cozy Bear Cottages in Bangor, Maine. I showed it to Alice and she just smiled, turned around, and headed to the bathroom. For a while her 2 p.m. crying sessions really bothered me, but I'm getting used to them. It's like when I broke my foot ice-skating. At first it hurt all the time, and then after a while it only hurt when I thought about it.

Hey, here's an idea. Maybe you could send me a letter sometime. It's hard to say much on a postcard. Oh! But don't get me wrong. I love the postcard! The brown bear mascot on the postcard is soooo cute—he reminds me of TB! I showed it to Millie and she thought he looked more like a grizzly bear than a stuffed animal. Shows you how much she knows!

Really, Millicent does have so much to learn. Today at the mall I bought a new pair of strappy Liz Price sandals. As we were leaving Sandberg's Shoe Emporium, I straightened up and whispered, "Millie, alert! Nine at two o'clock!"

"It's not two o'clock, it's four fifty-seven p.m."

"Noooo, there's a *nine* at *two o'clock!*"

"Nine what?"

"Millie, don't you know how to rate guys? This homeschooling business has really put a cramp in your social life."

Millicent looked pained and said, "Tell me something I don't know."

"Okay, how about nine stands for how a boy is rated, ten being the best, one, the worst. Two o'clock means that if we were standing in the middle of a giant clock facing the twelve, the boy would be standing on the number two."

"Is this a mathematical word problem?"

"Duh, nooooo. It's a highly sophisticated code for rating boys. You try it. What do you rate the one at nine o'clock?"

Millie examined him for a long time as if he were a science experiment. "A three?" she finally said.

"No, he's definitely a seven, or above. Try the two boys at eleven o'clock."

Millie locked her eyes on them. "A two for the one with brown hair, and a three for the one with the baseball cap."

"No way! I'd give the baseball cap an eight, and the buzz cut is a definite nine!"

After half an hour, Millie still had not rated anyone over a three. As we were scoping out the high school boys at four o'clock, I spotted Wendy from volleyball. She was with her mom, and they were both laughing really hard. Wendy's pretty, with short reddish-brown hair that she wears behind her ears, and she always has great earrings. She isn't one of those flashy girls. Instead, she's the kind that once you meet her, you wonder why you hadn't noticed her before, especially since she's so nice. Maybe that's why Julie doesn't pick on her. She doesn't see her.

"Hi Emily!" Wendy called out. "Hi Millicent!"

We both waved to her as she disappeared into Shah's department store.

Just then, I thought I saw the boy from the drugstore. "Hey! Is that him?"

"Him who?"

"You know."

"No, I don't."

"Yes, you do."

The boy turned and walked past us. Darn! It wasn't him.

"I thought it was the boy from the drugstore," I said. "How would you rate him?"

Millie made a face like something was smelly. "He doesn't even rate at all."

"Millicent! Really, what do you have against him? I'd give him a ten."

"Stanford Wong, a ten?" she croaked.

"Oops, not a ten," I corrected myself. "A twelve!"

"You're nuts," she yelled as she shoved me.

"You're nuts," I laughed as I shoved her back. "Stanford Wong? So he has a name after all! You held out on me! I give Stanford Wong a twelve-plus."

"Plus what? A dreaded disease? A lifetime of bad luck? A wretched odor serious enough to wipe out all humans, their pets, and most of the world's rodents?"

I interrupted Millie's rant. "So how do you know him? What can you tell me about him? Is he in our grade?"

"He's just Maddie's friend's grandson. That's all I know, okay?"

"Stanford Wong is hot! Stanford Wong is off the charts! Stanford Wong is better than the surfers of Solana Beach! Stanford Wong is —"

"Stop already!" Millie shouted, covering my mouth. "Enough of Stanford Wong! I'm sick of Stanford Wong!"

By the time we made it back to Millie's house, dinner was on the table — spaghetti with homemade sauce.

"I made the pasta," Mr. Min boasted as he served us. "Note that the noodles are different lengths. That's how you can tell they're homemade."

"I made the garlic cheese bread," Mrs. Min said as she slid an extra slice on my plate.

"I made the Boston cream pie," Maddie volunteered. She held up two noodles side by side and eyed them. "These look like the same size."

After a game of "Minopoly," Maddie said, "Come along, Emily. Even though you and Millie slaughtered us, I'll still give you a ride home."

Maddie drives a cool-looking old car. She claims her husband won it in a poker game. "And good thing he did. If he had lost, we would have had to hand over our Chinese camphor chest, twelve gold coins, and my wedding ring."

She held out her hand so I could admire her ring. I could barely see the diamond, but you could tell that she thought it was glorious.

"Maddie!" I yelled, covering my eyes.

"Oops," she said, putting both hands back on the wheel and swerving to miss a mailbox. "Yes, Millie's grandfather could pull quite a poker face when the odds were against him. You, on the other hand, would be better off taking your chances on the slot machines."

"What do you mean?"

"I mean you are very expressive, Emily. That's an admirable quality."

I felt my face flush. Was I that obvious?

"How's your mom doing?" Maddie put on her blinker and made a slow turn around the corner. I could hear the tires crunch on the pavement. "The last time you and Millie were over, you said Alice was acting strange."

"She still is. I dunno, she dresses in weird tie-dyed clothes and just works on the computer all the time. Alice says she wants to 'go with the flow,' then she gets upset if her files are out of order. She'll act all happy one minute and then sad or angry the next. If it weren't for her mood ring, I'd never know how she feels."

"Sounds like she doesn't know either," Maddie mused. "What about your father? Is he still on the road with the Tacky Boys?"

"The Talky Boys. Yep, he won't come back until after school starts."

"You miss him," she said matter-of-factly.

I was glad it was dark and Maddie couldn't see me. I'm trying so hard not to be a baby, but sometimes it feels like my heart is broken in two, and you and Alice each have one half.

By now this letter journal is pretty long. I can't wait until you read it. It's really weird, but now that we're far apart, I can tell you much more than when we were together. Millie says there's power in the written word. I wish I had the power to make you be here right now. I'm wearing your Members Only jacket, and I found half a roll of Cherry Life Savers in the pocket. I put it in a Ziploc bag to preserve it.

Love,
Emily

JULY 14

Dear Dad,

Alice was just sitting on the couch this morning staring at a flyer for Neighborhood Watch. It was spooky. Usually she's working in her office. But just sitting and staring? That's a new one.

Later, when I went to tell her I was going to Millie's, she wasn't in her office. So I went outside, but she wasn't there either. I ran back into the house and searched the entire first floor. I was out of breath by the time I raced upstairs. My jaw got all tense as I screamed, "Alice? Alice!" When I finally found her in the closet, I yelled, "Why are you hiding? That's so mean!"

She turned around, surprised. "Emily? I wasn't hiding, I was putting away clothes."

"You are so mean!" I shouted, storming off before she could make any more excuses.

After you and Alice had a fight, sometimes you'd be gone for days. Then when you two separated, I'd never know where you were for weeks. You'd never call. How come you never called? Once when I asked you about it, you just laughed and said, "You know me and phones. Phones are like a leash and I can't be tied down." Where did you go when you disappeared?

When I got to Millie's house, her parents were chasing each other around the yard. I thought it was hysterical, but I could tell this disturbed Millicent and she was pretending not to know them.

"Shall we eat at the mall?" I asked.

"Yes, please!"

After lunch at Taco Bell, we went to Shah's department store and looked at earrings. "Look, this pair matches our necklaces," I said, holding them up. "I think we'd better get them. My treat."

"I don't have pierced ears," Millie said.

"Well, you could get them pierced."

"Sure thing," she replied. "Right after I have my head examined."

As we left the store, I spied the photo booth. I dragged Millie over. "C'mon, it'll be fun!" We took tons of pictures.

"Millie, stop making faces and just smile!"

"This is my smile."

"It looks like you're in pain."

"This is how I look!"

"Like you just ate a lemon?"

"Emily, not everyone has a toothpaste-commercial smile like yours. Whenever I see a camera, I think my upper lip is going to get stuck on my teeth and I totally spaz out and turn to stone."

"Oh. Okay, never mind, it's okay," I said. Then, right before the flash went off, I tickled Millie. "Emily! Stop! Stop! Stop!" she hollered. "You're in big trouble!"

I didn't stop until Millie started smiling. We were laughing so hard that by the time the last flash went off, our stomachs ached.

"Wow," Millicent said, as she stared at the photos. "I wish my school pictures looked this good."

"I thought you were homeschooled?"

"Oh. I am." She looked away. "I wasn't always, though."

"What do you mean?"

"Nothing."

"No, tell me!"

"I used to go to public school," she mumbled. "But something happened and I don't go anymore."

She looked so sad.

"Millie, are you okay?"

"Tater Tots," she said softly.

"Excuse me?"

Millie walked over to a bench and plopped down. I sat next to her. She was quiet for a while. So was I. Then she said, "A lot of kids used to make fun of me. But there was this one boy who thought it would be funny to throw Tater Tots at me at lunch."

"How mean! Was it only once or did he do it a lot?"

"No, it was forever and it was awful, and everyone laughed at me. It wasn't just Tater Tots. Grapes, chicken nuggets, hamburger . . . whatever was on the menu ended up being on me."

"What did the lunch monitor do?"

"Nothing. I had to handle it myself."

I leaned in toward her. "Millicent, what did you do?"

She let a small smile cross her face. "I made a salt-shaker bomb."

"A bomb???!!!"

"A salt-shaker bomb. It doesn't hurt, but it foamed him and everyone laughed."

I grinned. She was amazing. "So he stopped throwing food at you! Brilliant!"

"Well, he stopped because I got kicked out of school." Millicent was quiet again.

No wonder she's homeschooled. It all makes sense now.

When I got home, I put the photos of Millie and me on the bulletin board you bought me last week. It has yellow material over it, and colored ribbons that crisscross so you just slide things under them and they never fall. I've got your postcards on it too, and some pictures of Nicole and A.J.

I feel so bad for Millicent. Clearly, it was hard for her

81

to tell me about that bully, but I am glad she did. I think we're better friends for it. True friends can be honest with each other without fear of being judged. If anything, I think more highly of Millie now that I know the truth about her homeschooling.

Love,
Emily

JULY 16

Hi Dad,

You're not going to believe this, but Maddie is moving to England! Get this: She's taking her husband's ashes because they were planning a trip there when he died. I think it's terribly romantic in a totally tragic sort of way. Maddie's going to go to school in London to learn how to arrange furniture. "Fung sway," it's called.

"This is crazy, she's crazy!" Millie just stared straight ahead as she devoured Cheeto after Cheeto.

Millie was in my butterfly chair and I was on the floor. Alice brought us some chocolate milk. "Emily, don't forget that our Neighborhood Watch meeting starts soon."

"Whatever."

"I'm sorry your grandmother's leaving, Millie," said

Alice. "Maybe she won't be away for long and you won't feel so bad."

I glared at Alice. What does she know about how someone feels?

"Thanks, Alice." Millie drained her glass and handed it back for a refill. "I just don't understand why she has to go. And why now?"

"Is there something that might prevent her from going? Is she in good health? Does she have the financial means?"

"Her health is fine, and she and Grandpa made a fair amount of money in tech stocks. Maddie consulted the tea leaves before any purchase or sale."

"So then, is there another reason she shouldn't go now —"

"Just stop!" I shouted. Millicent and Alice looked startled. "Millie and Maddie aren't some magazine article, Alice. This is real life. Maybe Millicent has some feelings that she doesn't want to talk about. Maybe her thoughts are private and personal, and not open to discussion."

"Emily —"

"What?"

"I'm talking to Millicent, not you."

We just glared at each other.

Millie stopped munching. "It's okay. No, nothing else is happening at the moment."

"Well," Alice said before she left the room, "if you ever need to talk to someone, you know where I am."

Millie gave her a sad smile. "Thank you, I appreciate that."

"What's wrong with me?" I asked when the door closed behind Alice.

"Nothing's wrong with you."

"No, I mean, if you need someone to talk to, you should talk to me."

"I do talk to you."

"I mean we're friends, right?"

Millie was silent for a moment. Suddenly I got nervous. What if she didn't consider me a good friend at all? I've misread people before.

"Emily," Millie said slowly, "of course we are friends. Really good friends."

"Really, really good friends."

"Yes, really, really, really good friends."

I hesitated. I hadn't even known Millicent for a month, yet it felt like I've known her my whole life.

"Millie, would you say we're best friends?"

Millie looked sort of spacey. Uh-oh. Why did I say anything?

"Best friends?" she stammered. "You want to be my best friend?"

I nodded and held on to my necklace.

She broke into a huge grin. "Okay. Yeah, sure. Why not? Yes! Best friends!!!"

"All right!" I shouted. I reached out to give her a hug, and she stiffened.

"I'm not one for hugging," she said, looking stricken.

"Well, we'll have to work on that then."

"Come on, Emily, time to go!" Alice called out. "Millicent, why don't you join us?"

"Get out while you can," I urged my best friend. "Run, run!"

There were ten adults, two plates of homemade cookies, one plate of veggies and dip, one plate of mini hot dogs, one package of Mint Milanos, and one kid at the Neighborhood Watch meeting in Mrs. Neederman's all-white living room. Her poodles barked the entire time, and everyone, including Mrs. Neederman, pretended not to hear them.

"Okay!" the policeman said. "We've got a good crowd, that's excellent. I'm Officer Joel Ramsey, and I'll be your Neighborhood Watch contact. For those of you who are not familiar with Neighborhood Watch, it is a crime prevention program. We enlist the active participation of good citizens like you who, in cooperation with law enforcement, are instrumental in reducing crime in communities like Rancho Rosetta. . . ."

Basically, it means that neighbors roam around with flashlights and spy on each other. I was more interested in looking at Officer Ramsey than listening to him. He looked like he could have his own television show. Well, okay, maybe not his very own show, but he could be on someone else's TV show. Even though he's sort of old (although not nearly as old as you or Alice), I'd give him an eight out of ten. At first he was a seven, then I gave him an extra point because of his uniform.

"I don't like guns," Alice was saying to Officer Ramsey.

Urrgggg, why does she always have to embarrass me?

"I don't either," he said. "Hopefully I'll never have to use one again."

Again? I wonder if he's ever killed someone? I studied him more carefully. As he told us more about totally boring Neighborhood Watch, he handed out brochures and stickers for our windows. I got an extra sticker for Millie since she was smart enough not to come with us. The door to her room is covered with warning labels and looks really cool.

I glanced at the sign-up sheet. "Why is my name on here?" I gasped.

"I put both of us down," Alice said. She passed the clipboard to Mrs. Neederman. "Neighborhood Watch is something we can do together."

"We do enough together already."

Alice smiled politely and said, tight-lipped, "Emily, not here and not now."

I moved my chair near the food table, slumped down, and gnawed on a carrot. One of Mrs. Neederman's poodles came over and stared at me. He started to bark, but stopped when I put the plate of mini hot dogs on the floor.

Alice is such a pain. Isn't it enough that she's dragged me across the country? Now she wants me to hunt criminals? It could be dangerous, life-threatening even. But does she care? Nooooooooooo. She doesn't care what happens to me at all.

Love,
Emily

JULY 18

Dear Dad,

Alice delivered the bad news today.

"Emily, we couldn't have held on to the Allendale house forever. It wouldn't be practical."

"Practical! Who cares about practical?"

"The house was bound to sell sometime, you knew that."

"How could it sell? The floors tilt, and the doors stick, and Dad never did get around to painting it. It would cost a fortune for anyone to fix it up."

Alice fiddled with the fringe on her blouse. "The new owners are going to knock the house down and build a new one in its place."

"What? And you're going to let them?"

"This is not my choice."

"Well, Daddy would never have let this happen. Does he even know?"

"He knows. His old boss sold the house for your father and called me today as a courtesy."

"I bet Dad didn't want to sell the house and you tricked him. This is all your fault."

"Emily! You think your father didn't want to sell the house? You think he wanted to keep it? It was his idea to sell. He wanted the money so that he could get new equipment and get the Talky Boys going again —"

"Stop it! You're lying. You wanted to get rid of the house so we could never go home again. You sold it so some strangers could knock it down and it would be like we were never there, like we never existed, like we were never a family!"

"Emily, your father sold the house, not me. He got it in the divorce settlement. I had nothing to do with it!!!"

"Not true!"

"Emily, listen to me. Emily, Emily, come back here. . . ."

I ran all the way to Millie's house, and rang and rang the doorbell. When no one answered, I went into the backyard and found Millicent in her tree house. The minute she saw me, she scrambled down.

"Emily, what's the matter?"

I tried to catch my breath before blurting out, "She sold it!"

"Oh no!"

"Oh yes! I was hoping . . . I was hoping that maybe someday . . ." I began to cry.

"It's okay, Emily." Millie ushered me into her room and handed me a tissue box.

"It's not okay. Alice doesn't trust me. Neither of them do. I didn't think they were really going to sell the house. Both of them acted like, 'Maybe we'll sell it, maybe we won't.'"

"But you said you hid the 'for sale' sign, so you must have known."

I sighed and began crying all over again. "I guess I hoped it really wouldn't happen. Just like the divorce, I knew they were thinking about it, but they never brought it up, so I thought that they changed their minds."

As I blew my nose, she opened the small safe in the back of her closet and pulled out a Hershey bar. "Even though the house may not be there," Millie said, "you can always hold on to the memories."

"You sound like Maddie," I said as I bit into the chocolate.

"Oh no!" Millicent cried in mock horror. "I sound like an old lady? Arrest me!"

On my way home I walked down Fair Oaks Avenue and put coins into the parking meters. It made me feel a little better. I wonder what you are doing right now? I'll bet you're as sad about the house as I am.

Totally depressed,
Emily

JULY 19

Dear Dad,

It's like we're pen pals, except you'll hear about my entire summer all at once and I'm getting your postcards every week or so. I keep wishing you'd call me, but Millie says, "If he wasn't a telephone person before, he's not going to suddenly turn into one now."

Will you do me a favor when your tour is over? Will you take some photos of our house before they knock it down?

I got your latest postcard and put a sticker on Syracuse. From the map, it looks like you're looping around now. The Comfort Z-Z-Zone Inn sounds really nice and restful. Do you get tired of being on the road, or is it fun? I think it would be fun not to have to make your bed every day. Millicent agrees with me and says that's why she sleeps in a sleeping bag on the top of her bed. She has a lot of really strange ideas. However, once you think about them they are totally logical.

"I know you're homeschooled and everything," I told Millicent, "so how do you make friends?"

"I have a few friends," she said. "Mostly, I meet people here and there. I had this one best friend, Debbie, but we finally figured that we didn't have that much in common."

"Friendships can get weird," I said, thinking of A.J.

and Nicole. I've barely heard from them. If they were true friends, wouldn't they have written to me more? Now Millie has moved up to be my number-one best friend. "Sometimes you think you are great friends with someone and then you are surprised to discover that you're not. That won't happen to us, though, right?"

"Right!" she answered.

I've told her about A.J. and Nicole, but not too much. I don't want her to feel bad that I have, *er*, had, other best friends that I'd known forever. She doesn't talk about her other best friends either. Even though it might not seem like it, Millicent is actually very sensitive.

It's strange, but A.J., Nicole, and I agreed on everything, and Millie and I disagree a lot. I used to think that if I had a totally different opinion from Nicole or A.J., they'd think less of me. I don't feel that way about Millicent. In fact, some of our best discussions have been disagreements. We can talk about anything and not have to worry about what the other person thinks.

We were in her room once arguing over what makes a guy attractive, and she named totally bizarre stuff like "high intelligence and a firm grasp of current events."

I wasn't sure if she was joking, so I told her my definition of "attractive." "Good hair, sparkling eyes, and the ability to make a person melt. You know, sort of like Stanford Wong."

"Spare me! You're not even close to accurate," she

said, reaching for one of her dictionaries. (She has four. That's one more than Alice. It's sort of sad that she needs so many.) "Let's look it up."

"Wait, I've got a better idea!"

We each made a list of our Top Ten Attributes for the Ideal Husband. (Millie came up with the title.) We didn't have one single overlap. How weird is that? At least we don't have to worry about getting engaged to the same guy.

"I always wanted to be like Sleeping Beauty or Snow White," I announced as Millie was still poring over her list. "You know, like one day my prince will come and carry me away."

"Well, wake up, Emily!" she barked. "You don't need some boy to rescue you. And if you think you're going to find a prince here in Rancho Rosetta, good luck. The only royalty in this town is Burger King, and his lineage is suspect."

Millie claims she's going to "hold off on marriage until I am a success in my chosen profession." I don't think I would wait. I'd be like you and Alice, except for the arguing and divorce part. I've heard of people who have divorced and then gotten remarried to each other again. Mrs. Min said that there's this famous actress, Tierney Turney, who married one of her husbands three times and took his name each time, so now her official name is Tierney Turney Turney Tarrantino Turney.

I can talk to Mrs. Min for hours. She loves to shop, and her idea of a dream vacation is the exact same one as mine — to go to the Mall of America. The other day as I was helping her fold sheets, she mentioned that they were having a sale on lotions at Body Beautiful. So today I brought her a present.

"What could this be?" Mrs. Min asked. "Orange blossom hand lotion! How lovely. Thank you, Emily, but you shouldn't have."

"Really," Millie added. "You shouldn't have."

I tried not to smile. "It was nothing," I said.

"Can I try some?" Mr. Min had been working on his latest project, building a combination microwave oven/CD player, and was holding a melted CD.

Soon we all smelled like oranges, except for Millie, who insisted her hands weren't dry. Later she asked, "Did you get some lotion for your mom too?"

It hadn't occurred to me to get something for Alice. She's still moping around in her dippy hippie clothes. Millie gave her a poncho yesterday. "Maddie says you can have it. She's been clearing out her things to get ready for her move to London. Her best friend made this, and she wants to make sure it has a good home."

"Why, thank you, Millicent!" Alice said. "Please thank Maddie for me too."

"Don't give her things like that," I hissed as Alice tried on the poncho. It got stuck over her head. "You'll just encourage her. She wants to act like she's all free-spirited, but she spent last night alphabetizing the medicine cabinet again."

Alice's head finally popped out of the top. She twirled around and said, "Millie, I can tell you're interested in journalism. Would you like to see one of the stories I'm working on?"

Soon I could hear them both chattering away about toxic mold. I'm not sure why Millie feels so obligated to talk to Alice all the time. She acts different around her too. Older. I think Alice has that effect on people. I heard you tell her once that she was making you grow up, and that you didn't want to. You said, "That's not who I am."

I guess now that Alice isn't around, you can go back to being yourself. I just wish you could be yourself and still be here.

Love,
Emily

JULY 20

Hi Daddy,

You called! You called! Millie said the odds were you wouldn't, but you did. It's like I sent you an ESP brain wave and you caught it, and you called!

I am soooooo sorry I wasn't home. If I had known you were going to call I would have been here, I promise. When Alice told me you called, I actually screamed.

"What did he say? What did he say?"

"He said, 'Hi Emily, it's Dad.'"

"What else? What else did he say?"

Alice sighed. "He said something like, 'I'm having a good time on the road. Hope you're having a great summer. Love you.'"

"Did he leave a number? I'm going to call him back right now!"

"No number."

"Why didn't you ask him for one?"

"Emily, he left a message."

"Why didn't you tell me that?"

I raced to the answering machine, but you weren't on it.

"ALICE!" I screamed. "The machine's broken. Dad's message isn't here. Alice, something's wrong!"

"I erased it," she said.

"You *what*???!!!"

I am so angry at Alice. I'll bet she erased it on purpose. It's like it's her mission to make my life miserable. Remember the times you took me out of school so we could go to Radio City and watch the orchestra practice? And then you'd talk to your musician friends while I got to wander around backstage? When Alice found out, she was so mad at us she just blew up and started yelling.

But even though we both got in big trouble, it was worth it.

Alice never took me anyplace fun. She always took me to school or the dentist or the doctor. I still remember the time you got your new convertible and we drove to New York City to go to Serendipity 3. I ordered a Frrrozen Hot Chocolate and you got one of those coffee drinks that come in tiny cups. We ran into your friend Margaret from the orchestra and she sat with us. She was so nice and funny. Afterward, you told me not to tell Alice about Serendipity 3 because it was so close to dinnertime and you'd get in trouble for spoiling my appetite. It was our secret and Radio City was our place, you said.

I hope, I hope, I hope you call again. Please call again, and if I'm not home be sure to leave a phone number and I'll call you back. I promise.

Love,
Emily

JULY 21

Hi Dad!

Guess what? On the oldies station they had a special called "One-Hit Wonders," and they played "Heartless Empty-Hearted Heartbreaker"!

When I heard it, I ran into Alice's office and she stopped working while we listened. It was very exciting! Afterward, the DJ said, "That was the smash hit from the Talky Boys! I wonder where they are now?"

"Their East Coast comeback tour!" I shouted at the radio.

Alice bought us new flashlights to use for Neighborhood Watch. I was sort of hoping we'd catch a criminal, but instead we just walked up and down, up and down the streets, shining our lights here and there.

"Isn't 'Heartless Empty-Hearted Heartbreaker' the best song you've ever heard?" I asked Alice.

"Yes."

Remember when your music used to make Alice happy? Now anytime I bring it up, it depresses her. It seems like the only thing she's into these days is her work. Well, that and trying to get me to buy into some sort of talk-fest.

"Emily, we should talk about the divorce . . ." she said after a while.

"Alice, let's not," I answered.

The totally bogus thing is, I sort of wouldn't mind talking to Alice now and then. Of course, it wouldn't be like when you and I talked about music and stuff like that. It would just be . . . I don't know. Talking. But I just can't bring myself to say anything to her. She tries too hard, and if I talked to her it would make her happy. For some reason, I can't stand the thought of her being happy. And she's kept things from me before, so why should I tell her every little picky thing about my life? Anyway, I'm still mad at her. Next time you call and no one's here, be sure to say, "Alice, DO NOT ERASE THIS MESSAGE!"

Hey, are you and the other Talky Boys enjoying your tour? Wouldn't it be cool if you played in Rancho Rosetta?

Remember when you always used to say I was like the fifth member of the band? I'd run errands, help pass out flyers, and sit in on your practice sessions. The other Talky Boys were always so nice to me, especially Luka. He would always let me play his drums. After you, Luka was the best musician, but you had TWO instruments, the guitar and your voice. I love it that you're the lead singer. I hope I get my singing talent from you and not Alice.

I remember when you suddenly started talking about the Talky Boys' big comeback. "Emily, it's going to be the real thing. Not just weddings and dances and low-paying stuff like that."

"But you liked playing at A.J.'s sister's bat mitzvah, right?"

"Right. But this is the big time. We're getting a manager and he's booking us in clubs! We'll tour the East Coast, and then if that goes well, we'll cover the whole country," you said. "It'll be just like before, when we could fill a stadium."

I just loved listening to you. You were so happy.

That's why I totally understood why you had to miss things like my school play when I was orphan number three, or when you couldn't make Parents' Night at school. What made me feel bad, though, was that you and Alice would always fight about it later. It bothered me that she used to get mad at you for not being around and spending time with me. If it was okay with me, why was it such a big problem for her? And her solution was what? A divorce, so I'd really never get to see you? Oh, that's smart thinking, Alice.

Luckily, there's nothing stopping you now. It must feel good to be able to focus on your music without any distractions. By the way, have you tried calling me back again? I'm sure you have, but to save money you probably hang up if it keeps ringing. I don't blame you. Long distance can be expensive.

Love,

Emily

P.S. I used the credit card to get a new MPS 5000 answering machine. The one we had was old and unreliable.

JULY 24

Hi Dad,

Millicent and I have decided that though volleyball is still horrid, it's not as bad as when we first started. I think it's because we have each other. Have you noticed that when there's someone else suffering along with you, it takes some of the pressure off? I told Millie that if I were ever being tortured to death, I'd want her right there next to me.

Though it's clear I will never be a professional volleyball player, I am getting a little better and can actually serve. I can't spike yet, but I am not bad at blocks. Millicent no longer closes her eyes when the ball comes toward her, and we both agree this is a huge improvement. So far our team is doing okay. Coach Gowin says, "We've lost about half our games." However, I prefer to think that we've won about half our games.

Win or lose, I always lead the team in a cheer at the end of every game:

> *Serve-ivors, Serve-ivors,*
> *We're number one,*
> *Go Serve-ivors, go Serve-ivors,*
> *Have some fun!*
> *SERVE-I-VORS!!!!*

I wrote that myself.

Julie hasn't been as scary lately. One time I even ran

into her at the mall and she said, "Nice Teddy + Joanie top." No matter what, I make it a point to smile at her, even though I used to imagine that she'd shrunk to the size of a volleyball. Millicent would throw her in the air for a set, and I'd spike her over the net. Oops! Did I actually write that? Bad Emily. Bad Emily.

Millie asked me why I'm always nice to Julie when it's clear our presence annoys her. "It's more work to be mean than it is to be nice," I explained. It's true. I've thought about this a lot. As I told Millicent, "It's not really worth the effort to scrunch up your face and send out bad vibes. Besides, scowling will give you premature wrinkles."

Alice is always talking about how the hippies loved everyone and everything. Though I try to block her out, some of what she says is sort of true. The world really would be a better place if we all got along.

I slept over at the Mins' again. I like it there. It feels like home.

"Lights out in five minutes," Millie's mom said through the closed door.

I pulled TB out of my sleeping bag and tugged on his nose. It's always getting smashed in. TB is starting to get pretty worn, but I keep telling him that he will always look wonderful to me.

"What is that thing?" Millicent asked, making a face.

"You know," I told her. "My bear. His name is TB. That's short for Teddy Bear. My dad gave him to me when I was little. It's TB's turn to sleep with me tonight."

"Are you aware that TB also stands for tuber-culosis?"

I ignored Millie. Sometimes she says things that are so random, I'm not sure how I'm supposed to respond. "TB is always here for me when I need him," I continued. "Who do you turn to when you're lonely? Do you have a favorite stuffed animal? Everyone needs a favorite stuffed animal."

Before she could answer, there was a knock on the door. "Come in!" I called out.

Mrs. Min started saying good night to us when she spied TB. "Oh, look at this adorable bear!" She picked him up and cradled him like a baby. "You know, I used to sleep with a stuffed animal when I was your age."

I could tell Mrs. Min would be the sort of person to appreciate stuffed animals. Alice still has Priscilla, that little brown bear you gave her when you were dating. Sometimes Priscilla's on her bed, sometimes she's in her office. Mostly she's in Alice's pajama drawer.

After Mrs. Min left, I asked again, "So, Millie, who do you turn to when you get lonely?"

A thousand hours later she declared, "I don't get lonely and I don't have any stuffed animals."

I didn't believe her.

Millie started to zone out. She does that a lot, like she's on another planet, and when she returns she's usu-ally a little bit sad. I knew something had to be done — and

fast. So I stood up, took a deep breath, and then *THUMP!*
The pillow smacked her hard in the face.

"Earth to Millie, Earth to Millie," I shouted.

"Hey!" She picked up her pillow and slammed me so
hard, I fell over backward.

"Oh no! Emily? Emily, are you okay?" I could tell she
was scared, so I pretended to be dead. I waited until
she was bent over me and shaking my shoulder. "Emily,
please say something!"

Suddenly I sat up and shrieked, "Ooooh, you are in so
much trouble," and started hitting her back with my
pillow.

Millie is a lot stronger than I thought she'd be. We were
both yelling and screaming and jumping on the bed when
one of the pillows popped. Just then the door opened.

Millicent and I froze as feathers filled the air. Mrs.
Min's jaw dropped, and I couldn't tell if Mr. Min was
angry or happy.

"I am so sorry," I said, trying not to make eye contact
with anyone. I was afraid I'd crack up.

"Me too," Millie giggled as she bowed her head.

"Not as sorry as you're both going to be in one minute!" Mr. Min stormed out of the room.

Soon he returned and shouted, "Prepare to die!"

Mr. Min broke into a huge grin as he tossed a pillow
to Mrs. Min, who caught it with one hand. Unbelievable.
They were joining in the pillow fight!

"Millie, here!" I shouted, throwing her a new pillow.

Millicent's parents were well trained in the art of pillow fighting. We were all laughing so hard that we started swallowing feathers and gagging. In the end, two more pillows popped before all four of us collapsed in hysterics. It was the best sleepover I've ever been to in my entire life.

Love,
Emily

JULY 25

Dear Dad,

I've got all of your postcards displayed in my room. Some are on my bulletin board and others taped to my walls. I like my latest one from Spree Lodge. The photo of the lobby looks so totally retro. I think it is great that you had two encores. Those fans in Buffalo really know a good band when they hear one!

Tonight Alice had to get right back to work after Stout's, so dinner was sort of rushed. She had another phone interview.

"Who are you talking to this time?"

"Oh, honey, I'd love to tell you, but it's confidential."

Later, as we were walking home, out of nowhere she

asked, "Emily, do you want to talk about how you feel about the divorce?"

"No," I answered. "I'd love to tell you, but it's confidential."

Alice doesn't even know I am writing this letter journal to you. If she did, she'd probably want to read it. She is so nosy. That's why she's a journalist, so she can poke into other people's business. She claims, "There are too many cover-ups in this world. I want my writing to be about the truth."

The other day I found a box filled with your photos under her bed. I put them up all around the house. The next day they were gone. Neither Alice nor I mentioned it. Because the truth is, we don't have anything to say to each other.

Love,
Emily

JULY 26

Hi, Daddy,

Even though Millicent told me she has summer school in the mornings, every time I bring it up she gets all weirded out, like it's a big shame. I'm starting to wonder if there's more to it than that. It's like when you'd just disappear.

I knew you were with the band. Still, sometimes I'd wonder.

"So, is it just English, or are you taking more than one class?"

"Just one," she said as she emptied the towels from the dryer in her room.

"You never said. . . . Why are you going to summer school if your dad homeschools you?"

"English isn't my dad's best subject," she mumbled.

"I think it's neat that he teaches you, but maybe your parents can talk the principal into letting you back in public school. That way we can both have someone to eat lunch with, and we can do our homework together. Wouldn't that be fun? We could have our own study hall. Oh, and we can join the Pep Club! Does the middle school have a Pep Club?"

"That would be great, but I asked my parents about it like you suggested, and they're convinced that I'm actually getting a better education right where I am."

"Alice says that Rancho Rosetta has one of the best public school districts in the nation. That's why we moved here. Maybe she can talk to your mom and dad about the middle school. She's sort of an expert on education. Right now one of the articles she's working on is about Shakespeare in inner-city schools. And get this — she expects me to read one of his plays, and I'm not even in summer school!"

"You don't want to read Shakespeare?"

"Uh, no. She says it'll be good for me to experience the world through literature, just like the kids she's writing about. I say, no thank you!"

Later, I talked to Millicent's dad about this as he was taking apart a toaster. "The Bard is not such a bad guy," Mr. Min assured me. He handed me a burned piece of Pop-Tart. Without thinking, I bit into it, then had to spit it out. "Reading can be a nice way to pass the time."

"Do you read much?"

"Me?" He started laughing. "Well, I'm not quite the reader that Millie and her mother are. But I have been known to pick up a book or two. I prefer nonfiction, like biographies and cookbooks. Or my favorites, biographies about chefs."

"You must have to read a lot to teach Millie."

"That's funny! Someone trying to teach Millicent something."

"But you do, when you homeschool her."

"Ouch!" Mr. Min cut himself on the toaster. I handed him a paper towel. "Oh yes. That homeschooling business. I have to teach her quite a bit. Now, this toaster is making me hungry. Let's round up Millie and go to The Scoop. There's a new flavor I want to try — Chocolate Caramel Pecan Parfait!"

The ice cream was great, plus later I had French silk pie at Stout's for dessert. Libby just automatically brings me a slice when we come in, so I didn't want to insult her by not eating it. Tomorrow I will eat extra fruit to balance things out. *Gamma Girl* says, "Eat great, eat healthy, but don't deprive yourself either."

"How's volleyball going, Emily?" Libby asked.

Alice looked up from her roasted chicken.

"It's okay." Why do people always ask questions the minute you put something in your mouth?

"Are the girls getting any nicer?"

"Yeah, I guess they are. They don't make fun of me or Millie as much anymore. Julie ignores us, which is fine with me. And I'm talking more to Wendy, that nice girl I told you about."

Wendy *is* nice. Today at volleyvall she told me, "Emily, I am so glad you're on our team. You make it so much more fun!" She turned to Millie. "I'm happy you're here too, Millicent. You're really improving. That last serve was so close to going over the net." Millie says Wendy doesn't have issues, like Julie does.

"Well, you keep it up!" Libby said. "Before long you'll have so many friends, you won't know what to do."

Alice stared at me as Libby walked away.

"Are you having any problems at volleyball?"

"No."

"Are some girls being mean to you?"

"No."

"Who's Julie?"

"No one."

"What's the matter? Did I say something wrong? Emily? Emily, talk to me."

Just as Alice was about to interrogate me some more, Officer Ramsey walked in.

"Alice!" he cried out.

Was she blushing? Alice was blushing.

"Officer Ramsey, you remember my daughter, Emily."

He had a wide grin as he reached out to shake my hand. "Of course. Hello, Emily! Will you be with your mom on Neighborhood Watch tomorrow night?"

I started to say something when Alice cut me off. "Yes, Emily and I will both be on guard to ensure the safety of our neighborhood!" She sounded like a total dork. "Joel, why don't you sit down and join us?"

Joel?

"I'd love to," he said as Alice slid over in the booth.

"No!" I shouted. Alice and Officer Ramsey both looked startled. "Uh, no. I mean, Alice, we need to talk." She just stared at me. "In private," I said.

"Oh, hey." Officer Ramsey stood up. "You know, maybe I'll join you two some other time. I'll just sit at the counter and read the newspaper and catch up on current events."

We watched him walk away.

"Emily? What is it you wanted to talk about?" She looked hopeful.

"Nothing."

"But you said . . ."

"Are you and Officer Ramsey good friends?" I asked.

"No."

"Do you hang out with him?"

"No."

"Do you want to?"

"Emily, please!" she whispered. "I barely know him. You're asking me too many questions."

That's a switch. I'm asking *her* too many questions? I can't believe I used to love talking to Alice. We talked all the time and you used to call us your "gabby girls," remember?

When you and Alice first separated, I didn't have much to say to either of you. And now I can't talk to you and I won't talk to Alice.

We ate the rest of our meal in silence. I could hear Officer Ramsey and Libby talking and teasing each other as she poured him a cup of coffee.

Don't worry, Dad. I'll keep an eye on Officer Ramsey for you.

Love,
Emily

JULY 28

Dear Dad,

The other day at the Beverly Aquatic Center, Mr. Min and I pretended to be synchronized swimmers. It was hysterical. Even the lifeguards were laughing, and a really buff one joined us. Later, I pretended to drown so he could save me. When he found out I was faking, I got a long lecture. It was totally worth it, though, because he had the most amazing hazel eyes. I wish the lecture could have lasted longer.

The only person who wasn't having a good time at the pool was Millie. She just dangled her feet in the water and refused to take off the huge T-shirt she was wearing over her bathing suit. Just as we were leaving, Julie and some of her friends arrived. They looked even skinnier in their bikinis, like they had lollipop heads. Julie glanced at me and said, "You should stay away from bright patterns."

Millie's eyes narrowed and she muttered, "And Julie should stay away from IQ tests."

I know Alice always tells me not to hate anyone, but I think I might hate Julie. Sometimes she seems okay, then out of nowhere, she'll say something mean.

On the way home, Mr. Min offered to take Millie and me to the movies. "There's a Looney Tunes festival at the Rialto."

"No thanks, Dad," Millie replied. "You've done enough for one day."

"He was just trying to be nice," I told Millie later.

"Yes, well, I think he ought to act more his age."

"I like the way he acts. He's fun, unlike Alice."

"Alice is fun," Millie jumped in. "I love talking to her. Emily, you have no idea how wonderful your mother is. Why do you ignore her?"

"I don't ignore her."

"Excuse me, but you pretend not to hear her when she talks to you, and when you do talk to her, you give her one-syllable answers."

"I do not."

"Do so. But when you're around my parents, you act all silly and funny and talk and talk and talk."

"Do you have a problem with that?"

"Noooo . . ."

"Because you talk and talk and talk with Alice, but whenever your parents want you to do something fun, you pretend not to hear them!"

Millie and I glared at each other. It was our first fight.

"I gotta go," I finally said. "I promised Alice I'd have dinner and do Neighborhood Watch with her."

"Okay, see you."

"Yeah, see you."

That night I was having a miserable time on Neighborhood Watch. Nothing ever happens. Plus I was feeling like the rainbow trout from Stout's didn't agree with me. Libby had said it was fresh, but I wasn't so sure. My stomach was acting all weird.

We kept walking up and down, up and down, up and down the street looking for "suspicious activities." I was wearing my new white Stephen Oliver shorts, my favorite Kirkpatrick Graffi-tee, the one with the monkey on it, and, as always, my friendship necklace. Just as we were about to head toward home, Alice screamed so loud that I started screaming too.

"Emily, oh Emily. Oh Emily!"

"What? What? A burglar???!!!"

She shined her flashlight on my shorts.

At first I didn't get it. I thought I had been shot. Then I realized. It had started. I had started. I had started my — my — you-know-what. My "time of the month."

"Oh, sweetheart," Alice said, wrapping her jacket around my waist and giving me a hug. "My little girl is growing up. This is major. "

"Can we *please* just get out of here?"

Just then, Officer Ramsey drove up. When he saw us, he flashed the red light on top of his police car. I could have died.

"Didn't mean to scare you, Emily," he said as he leaped out. "Hello, Alice, anything new to report?"

"You'll never guess," Alice said. *Ohmygosh, she's going to tell him.* "Everything appears quiet in Rancho Rosetta!"

"Just the way I like it," he said. "I had enough commotion when I worked for the Secret Service."

"I didn't know you worked for the Secret Service. I'd love to hear more about that." *Not now, not now, not now!* "But perhaps some other time. Emily and I were just heading home."

"Then hop in," Officer Ramsey said, opening the car door. "I'll give you a lift."

Normally, I would have been thrilled to ride in a police car, only this time I was a bit preoccupied.

"You need to wear your seat belt, Emily," Officer Ramsey said.

"Uh, sure. Okay."

Luckily, the trip home was only a couple blocks. As Alice and Officer Ramsey said their good-byes, I ran into the house. Just as I finished changing my clothes, Alice appeared.

"Emily, we need to talk."

No, we didn't need to talk. Why does she always want to talk? Alice started getting all weepy. "You're not a baby anymore!"

"Alice, I haven't been a baby for a long time."

This made her cry even more. I felt good and bad at the same time, but mostly bad. She looked so confused that all of a sudden I started crying too. What was happening to my body? To me?

"It's okay, Emily. It's okay," Alice said. "Come on, dry those tears. We have some shopping to do!"

Shopping?

At the drugstore I was stunned by the number of "products." I had always hurried past Aisle 14, but tonight I had to slow down and even stop. For once I was glad Alice was with me.

"We'll need these, and these, and this," she said, tossing packages into my basket. "Did we miss anything?"

How was I supposed to know? I picked up a couple of boxes that had nice flowers on them and added them to the pile.

"I need a few things for myself," Alice continued. "Why don't you treat yourself to a candy bar, and I'll meet you at the checkout?"

As I was trying to decide between a giant Hershey bar and a box of Milk Duds, *he* walked into the store. Stanford Wong! The boy who set off the alarm. The boy with the lopsided smile. The boy whose Zappo Zit I sleep with under my pillow. There he was, not more than six feet away from me, and I was holding enough feminine hygiene products to fill twelve medicine cabinets.

Before he could see me, I ditched the basket and ran out the emergency exit, setting off the alarm.

About half an hour later, Alice showed up at home. "Where did you go?" She looked worried. "I searched everywhere for you. I found the basket just sitting in the middle of the aisle. You know you shouldn't have left without telling me. Emily, sometimes I just don't know about you." She slowed down when she saw how upset I was. "Well, I suppose you're a little confused right now. I don't blame you. In some countries this is a rite of passage that calls for a big celebration. Shall we have one?"

"Uh, no."

The more Alice droned on, the more confused I got. Things are changing. I am changing, and I am not sure if I like what's happening to me.

Love,
Confused Emily

JULY 29

Dear Dad,

Alice was really, really nice to me last night. Usually she's all tense about work or whatever and is either spacing out or spazzing out. But last night we both just chilled. She served me tea and we watched television. Alice did try to start a discussion about my period, but I said, "Not now," and for once she didn't push.

I called Millicent today. I wasn't sure if I should, since our last conversation was sort of weird and I didn't know if we were still mad at each other. But I really needed to talk to someone who was not Alice. Millie was waiting for me at our table in the mall. She handed me a chocolate shake, then took a sip of hers.

"What is it that you couldn't even hint at over the phone?" she asked, trying to sound casual.

I could tell she was dying of curiosity. Millicent can't stand not knowing things. If you ever want to bug her, just say, "I had something really important to tell you, but I forgot what it was."

I didn't know how to tell her my news, so I stirred my shake with the straw and began, "There comes a time in every girl's life that . . ." Millie looked confused, and I realized I was sounding very Alice-ish. So instead I blurted out, "I started my period!"

Millicent was speechless, and so were the man and his teenage son at a nearby table. As Millie and I walked through the mall, I told her all about how I was feeling, and how I felt sort of powerful, but sort of scared at the same time. I love how Millicent was there for me when I needed her. She's a good listener.

I would tell you more about our conversation, but I don't want to gross you out. Boys are so lucky they don't have to go through stuff like this. It's not really fair. Life is so easy for boys.

Love,
Emily

JULY 30

Dear Dad,

Alice is still insisting I read some Shakespeare play, so today I went to the library. I had walked past it plenty of times but had never gone inside. Alice kept telling me what a great library it was, and now I know why. Books filled the dark wooden shelves, bright artwork lined the walls, and a miniature castle rose up in the middle of the children's department. A castle — how cool is that?

As I was looking at the magazines, I heard a familiar voice say, "Stop that, you're being impossible!" I turned the corner and could not believe what I saw.

"Ohmygosh, Millie, what are you doing here? I just came to get my library card. And . . ." I stopped when I saw someone look at me from under the table. "Uh, hello down there! I'm Emily, Millie's best friend. I don't think we've met."

The boy leaped up and began shaking my hand. It was *him*. The boy from the drugstore. What was he doing under Millie's table? I turned to her for some answers, but she looked as surprised as I was. Before either of us could say anything, the boy opened his mouth.

"Stanford Wong," he boomed. "I'm just, uh, uh . . . I'm just helping Millicent here with her studies." I heard Millie yelp, but Stanford kept going. "Uh, this is a superfine library. Really nice."

"It really is nice," I told him. *He* was really nice.

"Yes, so true. Even the bottoms of the tables are clean. Uh, that's why I was under the table, I check the tables' tops and bottoms for cleanliness."

"Oh, so you're some sort of table monitor?" I joked.

"Uh, unofficially, yes," he joked back, grinning.

It was like Stanford Wong and I were totally in sync. I could feel waves of in-sync-ness swirling around us like we were in the eye of a tornado. If I was ever in a natural disaster, Stanford is who I'd want to be with. He was even better-looking than I remembered.

"Excuse me!" Millie interrupted. I was startled to find her standing next to me. "We really should be getting back to the books."

I frantically tried to signal Millicent to leave Stanford and me alone, but before she could respond, Stanford spoke. "Um, Emily, I'm sure Millicent would prefer it if you weren't here during our tutoring sessions." He looked totally heart-stopping as he lowered his voice. (Stanford has a *really* great voice.) "She gets embarrassed. Of course, if Millicent ever figures out the difference between plot and theme, then maybe we could all get together afterward. You know, get a burger or something."

"Oh! That sounds like a terrific idea. Stanford, we'd love to go."

I glanced at Millie. She looked ill. How insensitive could I be? I knew exactly what she was thinking. I took her aside. "It's okay, Millie. This explains a lot of things, like why you disappear sometimes. Your English class must be really hard if your dad can't teach you. But even though you're homeschooled, you shouldn't feel bad if you need extra help." Millicent just stared at me with her mouth hanging open. "Not everyone can be a genius, but I don't think any less of you because Stanford has to tutor you. Truly, there's nothing wrong with admitting that you're not the smartest person on the planet. In fact, I think you're very brave to ask for help."

I could see Stanford watching us. He seemed very concerned about Millicent. "Stanford's waiting," I told her. She winced. "You'd better get back."

It must have been some really hard assignment. As I roamed around the library, I could see Millie arguing with Stanford, and at one point I witnessed an eraser bouncing off his head.

Ms. Martinez was at her desk, circling books in a magazine. Her hair looks naturally wavy and black, and she's really nice and youngish. She helped me select *Romeo and Juliet*. From the way Ms. Martinez described it, it actually sounded good, plus it wasn't as long as *Hamlet*. I squeezed into the castle in the children's department and was about to open the book when Stanford peered into the window.

"Hey, Emily, we're quitting early, so now we can go to Burger King!"

Burger King was sooooo fun. I feel like I've known Stanford forever. He's just as funny and nice as he is cute.

Remember when I rated him a twelve out of ten? I want to change that to a fifteen! A twenty! A forty!

"Emily, do you miss New Jersey?" he asked as he took a bite of his hamburger.

"Yes, well, some things," I confessed. "We used to live in this creaky old house and our backyard was on the edge of the woods. I loved that house."

"Well, um, I'm glad you moved here."

"You are? Stanford, what a nice thing to say. Are you always this nice?"

I glanced at Millicent. She looked bored, so I switched the subject to volleyball so she could participate in the conversation.

"Volleyball's a good sport. I play basketball." Stanford held up his ball as proof.

"Are you any good at it?"

"I'm on the A-Team. It's the first time a seventh-grader is on the A-Team."

"Wow, Stanford, so you're on the A-Team and you're really smart too? That's a double whammy."

Millie looked up from her French fries. She had lined them up side by side according to size. "Stanford smart?"

"Well, yes. After all, he's tutoring you, isn't he? He wouldn't be a tutor if he weren't smart. Right, Stanford?"

Both Millicent and Stanford suddenly went silent. I wondered if I had said something wrong. Stanford stood up. "Excuse me," he said.

"Gosh, Millie," I whispered as we watched him walk

away. "Stanford's cute and smart and athletic. What more could you ask for?"

"Someone of our own species."

He came back with two fistfuls of straws, but Millicent shamed him into putting most of them back. I don't know why she doesn't like him. Maybe she feels awkward around him because he's her tutor.

Stanford returned this time wearing a Burger King crown. "Here's one for each of you," he said. I put mine on immediately. Millicent just tossed hers on the table and rearranged her French fries. Then when Stanford was showing us a really funny trick where he pressed a napkin up against his face and stuck his tongue through it, Millie bolted out the door. Sure, it was gross, but not that gross. I had to run to catch up to her.

"What's the matter? Did I say something wrong? Millie? Millie, talk to me."

Millicent started to say, "The tu . . . tutoring . . ." but choked on her words.

Of course! Oh, how stupid I had been. "You're still feeling bad because I found out that he's tutoring you. It's okay, really it is. Millie, we're best friends, remember? Nothing can come between us, okay? Come on back and join us." I picked up her briefcase. It was really heavy. "Stanford claims he can put a whole Whopper in his mouth at once!"

"No, you go ahead," she insisted as she wrestled the briefcase from me. "I have a lot of stuff I need to do."

"Are you sure?"

"Yeah, go on without me."

"Well, okay then . . ." I waited for her to change her mind, but she didn't. "You're sure you won't join us?"

"Positive!" Millie said brightly.

"All right then. See you tomorrow, I guess."

I felt funny going back to Burger King alone. Something didn't seem quite right with Millie. Really, what difference did it make that she had a tutor? Although I *would* have liked to have known that her tutor was *Stanford Wong.*

"Where's Millicent?" Stanford seemed happy to see me.

"She went home. I just don't know about her sometimes. Stanford, please make me a promise." A strange look crossed his face.

"Are you okay?" I asked. "All of a sudden you look weird."

"I was, uh, just trying not to burp."

"Oh! Listen to this!" I'm not sure what came over me, but I took a huge gulp of air and then burped out the words, "Hello, Stanford!"

Instantly, I regretted it. *Stupid, stupid, stupid.* Stanford stared at me and then said, "Wow, Emily, you're just too cool." I felt myself blush until his eyes went to my second cheeseburger. "Uh, are you going to eat that?"

Ohmygod. He thinks I'm some sort of pig, I can just tell. I knew I should have just ordered one cheeseburger. "You think I eat too much, don't you?" I heard myself ask. "You think I'm fat."

Stanford turned red. "No, no, no," he insisted, shaking his head. "Not at all! I just thought that if you weren't going to eat it, I'd help you."

I exhaled, took a bite, and then handed it over to him. There was a moment when we were both touching the burger. It was so romantic. As he bit into it, Stanford asked, "Uh, was there something you wanted to talk about?"

I remembered Millicent. "Please promise you won't make fun of Millie for being so bad in English. You know, not everyone's as smart as you are."

Stanford nodded and wrinkled his forehead in the cutest way. "It's not nice to make fun of a person just because they don't get good grades," he said. "Grades aren't everything. Sometimes a person's feelings are more important than a stupid grade!"

"Stanford, you are amazing." He really is.

"Yes, well, let's be a good friend to Millie and respect her privacy."

I was so moved I almost began to tear up. He must have sensed how emotional I was, because just then, he picked up his Coke and stuck the straw straight into his nostril! We both really cracked up over that, and when he did it again, I almost spit out my soda.

Stanford's not like any other boy. He really listens, and he looks at me when I talk. I heard that if a boy *like* likes you, his pupils dilate. But every time I tried to examine Stanford's eyes, he was already staring at me, and I'd suddenly feel shy and start blinking a lot.

As the afternoon wore on, we talked about everything. No topic was off-limits.

Transportation: "Your dad drives a red convertible Alfa Romeo Spider? That's a total rock star car! Man, my dad's just some boring lawyer."

Emergency rooms: "Really, Stanford? But what was the peanut doing in your nose in the first place?"

Fashion: "I consider myself fashion-forward, but not obsessed with it too much. Well, just a little. I can look at any outfit and nine out of ten times identify the designer."

Sports: "Basketball is my life."

And even religion: "I'm half Jewish and half not Jewish," I explained. "My mom is Jewish and my dad's sort of Catholic. When they got married it's like their religions canceled each other out. We hardly ever went to church or to temple, although Alice keeps hinting that she'd like to start going again."

"My best friend Stretch is Jewish," Stanford mused.

"Does he talk about it much?"

"No."

"Oh. What are you?"

"I'm Chinese American."

"I meant, are you religious?"

"I used to go to church all the time with my grandmother, but she doesn't get out much these days. I do pray a lot during basketball games, though."

We stretched the day out as long as we could. While Stanford ate two more hamburgers, an order of onion rings, a soda, and two shakes, I nibbled slowly on my French fries and had another Coke.

"Well," Stanford said, finally standing up and reaching for his basketball. "Uh, I guess I'd better head home or I'll be late for dinner."

"Oh. Yes, me too."

We were both still wearing our crowns.

"So, Emily, maybe I'll see you again sometime."

"Okay, when? I mean, yes, I hope so. I'd like that."

When I floated into the house, Alice looked up at me and smiled. Instantly I hit Earth and raced to my room. I didn't want her asking me any questions.

It's been four hours and thirty-seven minutes since I last saw Stanford Wong. I am wearing my crown right now. It will make a nice addition to my collection. I also saved my drink cup and even managed to sneak one of Stanford's napkins. Would it be too much, I wonder, if I had it laminated?

Forever,

Emily

AUGUST 1

Dear Daddy,

I hate going to the dentist. This new one is nice, but still, I hate going to the dentist. Dr. Jill kept talking to me while she was digging around in my mouth. The amazing thing was that she could totally understand what I was saying. I wish you and Alice could understand me as well as she could. But then, I don't understand you two either.

Alice modeled a new outfit for me tonight. "This is a dashiki. It's an African garment," she said proudly. "It is so comfortable. I love the bright colors. Do you like it? I could get you one."

"No thank you," I told her as I backed away. "Why can't you dress like a normal person?"

"A normal person? Define 'normal,' Emily."

"I don't know. Like Mrs. Min, or someone your age."

"You want me to act my age, is that it? What about your father?" Her voice started rising. "You don't seem to have a problem with him, and he's acting like a twenty-year-old, running around with a band! Tell me, should he act his age too?"

"All right, all right. Forget it! Forget I even said anything! Dress however you like, see if I care!"

I retreated to my room and listened to "The Emily Song" a few times. That always calms me down. Then I reached for the self-tanning gel. It was featured in *Gamma Girl*, so it must be good. According to the magazine, "The tan may be fake, but our model Betina looks natural."

Remember the last time we went to the beach? We lost track of the time and I turned a bright, crispy red. It hurt soooooo much. When we got home, Alice had to rush me to the emergency room. No more Mr. Sunshine for me. Tans from a bottle are it for now!

After I waited an hour for the gel to dry, I put on my orange Castellucci Collection sundress and my friendship necklace. Then I sprayed myself with Bubbly Beautiful, just in case I ran into someone special.

I recognized Millie's bike in the library parking lot. It's blue and has a handmade license plate that reads 2BRN2B. As I pushed the heavy library door open, I held on to my necklace for good luck.

In the far corner of the room I saw Stanford Wong slouched so far down in a chair he was almost on the floor. He sat straight up when he saw me and sent me a huge grin, which I returned a million times over. Millicent was with him. I gave them a small wave as I headed in their direction, even though what I really wanted to do was jump up and down.

Stanford and I gazed at each other so long that I was startled when Millie cleared her throat and said, "Emily, we're nearly finished here. I thought we were meeting at your house?"

Without taking my eyes off of Stanford, I said, "I wanted to make it easier for you, so I came here. I'll just wait over by the magazines until you're done. Bye, Stanford."

"Bye, Emily."

I pretended to be reading a book about the Lakers, Stanford's favorite basketball team, while the two of them finished up a spirited debate about homework.

Ms. Martinez came up to me, carrying an armload of books. "Hello, Emily! How's *Romeo and Juliet* coming along?"

I was too embarrassed to tell her I hadn't started it. So instead, I said, "Um, that William Shakespeare was some great writer."

From where I was, I could see Millie packing up to leave. Before I could get to Stanford, Millicent rushed me out the door. It would have been too obvious to yell, "Stanford, follow me!" So I just waved good-bye and sent him ESP brain waves that said, "I want you to come with us, but Millie is in a hurry. However, I hope we will see each other soon."

Once outside, Millie hopped on her bike and shouted, "Come on, Emily. Let's get out of here!"

"Slow down!" I shouted. "Millie, what's your hurry? Where are we going?"

"To Maddie's. I promised her I'd stop by for scones."

"Scones? Why don't we stay at the library? Maybe Stanford wants to talk to us —"

"Stanford Wong does not want to talk to *us*!"

"Maybe he likes scones," I yelled as I ran to keep up with her. "Maybe we should invite him to Maddie's."

Millie hit the brakes on her bike and skidded to a stop. "Emily, Maddie invited you and me, not Stanford. Okay???!!!"

I sighed. "Okay. But maybe we can do something with Stanford some other time."

"Urrgggg," was all Millie said.

The scones were delicious. This time Maddie served chocolate-chip ones with an orange glaze. We all spoke with British accents as we ate, but Maddie was the best at it. She's been practicing, she says.

When I got home there was another postcard waiting for me! I like the photo of the Comfort Motel. It's really cool the way they got all those trucks to line up in the parking lot. Erie, Pennsylvania. Erie sounds sort of spooky — is it? I'm sorry the club messed up and didn't get the ad in the paper on time. I'm sure that's why it wasn't a sellout. And it's too bad that Luka snores. I guess you're sharing rooms now? Maybe you could ask him to wear a Silent Knight Snore Fighter. I saw an infomercial for one and they work really well.

After your tour ends, will you come visit me in Rancho Rosetta? Please, please, pretty please. You can have your own room and I'll show you around town. First, we'll go to Mel's for hot dogs smothered in chili and cheese, and we'll wash them down with orange frost freezes. After that I'll take you to Zooi's Zowie Music-teria. The man who owns it has a ponytail. Mr. Zooi says he was a huge fan of the Talky Boys. One time he even went in the back of his shop and brought out a poster. He shook off the dust and unrolled it.

"That's Luka in the sandbox, and Dean, aka Mr. McCoy, on the swings, and Dayton hanging upside down on the monkey bars. And that's my dad," I said proudly, "on the slide."

"You have the same eyes," Mr. Zooi commented.

Hear that? We have the same eyes!

After the Music-teria, we'll go to Maddie's house and she'll teach us some yoga, or read our tea leaves, or tell us about the times she's been arrested. Sometimes she even reenacts her arrests. It's so cool, especially when she shouts, "Cause and Effect!" Then we'll hit the Rialto for a movie. When that's done, we'll head to Butterfield's Bakery for cookies or to The Scoop for ice cream before we visit the mall to go shopping. Then for dinner, we'll see what Libby has on the menu at Stout's. Plus, who knows? Maybe we'll bump into Stanford Wong and I can introduce the two of you and you can talk about your car.

I just know you're going to love Rancho Rosetta! In fact, you'll probably love it so much, you'll never want to leave.

Love,
Emily

AUGUST 3

Hello, Dad!

I couldn't find Millie before volleyball, so I went to Maddie's in search of her. Millicent has lots of sleepovers at her grandmother's house. They stay up late and eat junk food and watch old movies. The first person to fall asleep has to cook breakfast for the other person. Maddie always makes glazed doughnuts with sprinkles that Millicent says are really from Benny's Doughnut Palace. Millie always toasts Pop-Tarts "fresh from the box."

"Millie? Let me check," Maddie said, motioning me inside. She lifted the cushions off the couch, peeked behind the curtains, and looked under Julius. "Nope, Millie's not here. But sit down. I just baked some cookies and I need someone to share them with."

I could hear her knocking around the kitchen, then, with a great flourish, she came back balancing four tall stacks of Oreos on a plate.

"Uh, you made these?"

"Yes, aren't they round?"

I reached for one and unscrewed the top, the way you always do.

"So!" said Maddie, reappearing with two champagne glasses of milk. "What kind of mischief are you and Millie up to these days?"

"No mischief."

"Oh." She sounded disappointed.

"But Millie did tell me the truth about what she's doing this summer."

Maddie perked up. "Millicent told you?"

I took apart a second Oreo and ate the middle. "I was surprised, but I'm glad I know. I'm not sure why it was such a big secret in the first place. I mean, why would she think I'd even care about her grades?"

"Well, some people are funny about that."

"I'm Millie's best friend. You'd think she'd know that I would like her no matter what."

"You're a good person, Emily Ebers," Maddie said, taking my hand and slipping an Oreo into it.

"I'm not sure what the big deal about summer school is, or why she didn't want me to know about this tutoring business. How long has Stanford been tutoring Millie?"

"Excuse me?"

"How long has Stanford been tutoring Millie?" Maddie hesitated before picking up another Oreo. "You do know that he's tutoring her, don't you?" I hoped I hadn't spilled Millicent's secret.

Maddie slowly bit into her cookie, not even bothering to unscrew it. "Is that what she told you?"

"Well, I came across the two of them at the library, and Stanford told me. Do you know him? Stanford Wong."

"He's my best friend's grandson. Good boy, that Stanford Wong. Excellent penmanship. He's very kind to his grandmother."

"Is there any chance that Millie likes him, you know, as more than a friend?"

Maddie let out a hearty laugh. "As much as Stanford's grandmother and I would love that, it just isn't happening. As it is, the two of them fight like brother and sister, which is too bad because he's really a very nice boy."

"Yes! That's what I keep trying to tell Millicent, that Stanford's really nice. But no matter what I say, I can't convince her." Just then Maddie's clock started cuckoo-ing. "Oh no, I'm late for volleyball! Gotta go, thanks for the snack."

"Come back again soon," Maddie called after me as I ran down the sidewalk. "Next time I'll make Twinkies!"

Millie was already at volleyball practice, which was no surprise. What did surprise me, however, was seeing Stanford Wong sitting in the bleachers. Julie and her backup singers kept looking at him and giggling. If he noticed them, he didn't act like it. I pretended not to notice them noticing him. Millie did too.

It seemed like everyone tried harder because Stanford was watching. After every point, win or lose, the entire Serve-ivors team, except for Millicent and Coach Gowin, turned to him for a reaction. The game was close, but Wendy scored the winning point. I was so happy I gave her a huge hug and couldn't stop jumping up and down.

"Serve-ivors rule!" I shouted, as the others joined in my cheer. "Go Serve-ivors! Go Serve-ivors!"

Coach Gowin smiled. She's not nearly as scary when

she smiles. "See what a little teamwork can do? Good game, girls. Dismissed!"

I took off running toward Stanford. It wasn't until I was halfway up the bleachers that I realized what I was doing. By then there was no turning back. So I just pretended I meant to be running, and when I got to Stanford I said, "Hmmm, that wasn't my fastest time up the bleachers, but it was close." I was horrified when I looked at my wrist and realized I wasn't wearing a watch. Luckily Stanford didn't seem to notice.

"Hi, Emily!"

"Hello, Stanford."

We gazed at each other forever, until someone screamed, "EXCUSE ME! Are you even on this planet?"

How long had Millie been standing behind me, I wondered? I was glad she was there. If I ran up to Stanford alone it might be too obvious that I *like* like him. It's clear he knows that I like him, but does he know how I really, totally, and truly feel? And does he just like me, or does he *like* like me too?

"I was thinking that we should get ice cream. I really like ice cream. Do you like ice cream, Stanford? It's very refreshing on a hot day, or a cold day, or most days."

Must stop blathering.

"Ice cream? I love ice cream!" he said.

"I'm glad they invented ice cream."

"Me too!" Stanford agreed. "Whoever invented it should get a trophy or have a holiday named after them."

"Millicent, do you like ice cream?" I heard Millie mutter to herself. "Well, yes, thank you for asking. Yes, Millicent, I do like ice cream."

As we made our way down from the bleachers, I almost fell, but Stanford caught me. He's very strong.

"Thank you . . . Stanford."

I like saying his name out loud.

"You're welcome . . . Emily."

I felt faint and considered falling again. I could see Wendy and the other girls staring at us. Julie looked particularly stunned and didn't say a word as we walked past her.

As the three of us headed to the ice-cream parlor, Stanford and I talked nonstop. He opened the door for me, and when it was my turn to pay, he stepped in front of me and said, "I've got this one covered." That must mean he *like* likes me, right? He didn't offer to pay for Millie's. She pointed this out later as a sign of his rudeness, although I argued that his paying for my cone was a sign of his generosity.

As we ate, Stanford told me how his free throw won the league championship. I barely heard him, because I was too busy staring at his eyes, and his mouth, and his nose, and his ears, and his hair. Sigh. He's so totally hot. I wonder if a smart jock like Stanford Wong could really fall for a slightly-heavy-blond-brown-haired-poor-volleyball-playing girl like me? Maybe he's just nice to everyone.

As we got to the bottoms of our ice-cream cones, I tried to put off finishing mine as long as possible. I think Stanford did too. We both nibbled the tips of the cones, even though Millie had finished hers a long time ago and was now standing up and saying in a very loud voice, "Well, Stanford, such a pleasure seeing you, but now, sadly, we must be leaving. Come on, Emily, let's scram."

Later, at Millie's house, I asked, "Do you think he likes me? I mean, do you think I even have a chance with someone like him? He's probably had millions of girl-friends, and I've never had a single boyfriend, except for Evan in kindergarten, but that doesn't really count. I wonder if Stanford came to watch Julie play volleyball. Maybe she's the one he's interested in. . . ."

Millie put both fingers in her ears and began to hum. "Hmmmmmmmmm, hmmmmmmmm. I can't hear you!" Then she flopped over onto the floor and didn't move.

"Millie? Millie, are you okay?"

Still facedown on the rug, she said in a muffled voice, "Emily, your incessant chatter about Stan-Turd has finally bored me to death."

"I'm sorry, Millicent," I said, laughing. "What do you want to talk about?"

"I want to talk about anything but Stanford Wong!"

"What is it about him that you hate so much?"

"I don't hate him," she said, as she sat up and buried her nose in an Archie comic.

"It sure seems like you do."

Millie was silent for a moment, before saying, "He's just such a jock. A mindless boy. And he represents all that I detest in a human being. However, if you choose to like him, then be my guest."

Oh, Dad, I wish you were here! You could tell me how a boy thinks. Their brains are so mysterious, it's like they're from another planet. A.J. says that the way you can tell if a boy *like* likes you is if he totally ignores you, no matter what. Even if you stomped on his foot while holding a bucket of cheeseburgers and a monkey, he would act like you're not even there. And the more he ignores you, the more he likes you.

Nicole claims that if a boy *like* likes you, he would tell you that you're stupid, but smile while he said this. If he's the quiet type, he might throw something at you like a wad of paper, or try to steal your food at lunch. And if the boy is in total *like* like, he'll try to impress you by not acting like himself.

I think that the only real way to tell if a boy *like* likes you is to be direct. None of this game-playing, that's juvenile. Instead, even though it might be scary, the thing to do is to just march right up and ask one of your friends to ask someone else to ask one of his friends what he thinks about you.

Unfortunately I don't know any of Stanford's friends, and I only have one friend here, and she's not exactly trying to be helpful.

"Millicent," I said. She was still engrossed in the comic. "Maybe you could ask Stanford if he likes me."

"Why would I want to ask him that?"

"Because I need to know."

"So you ask him."

"I can't do that. What if he says no?"

"Then you'll have your answer."

Urrggg!!! Sometimes Millie just doesn't get it.

Okay. Well, enough of Stanford for the moment. I still have his Zappo Zit — I keep it with your aftershave. I sleep with the Burger King crown under my pillow now. At first I didn't want to smash it, but now I don't mind. It was something he gave to me. I also kept the wrapper from the ice-cream cone he bought me today. I'm going to put everything in a special box.

Alice has a whole box filled with things from you, like ticket stubs from the Wild Youth concert, and the Superman Pez, and even that song you started writing for her but never finished. Maybe as a surprise you could finish it. Evan used to always say, "My parents get along better now that they're divorced than when they were married."

Maybe now that you and Alice are divorced, you can try to be friends.

Love,

Em

AUGUST 4

Dear Dad,

Remember how many times I used to watch *Snow White* when I was little? I watched it again this morning and it was so romantic, except that she was basically dead when the prince kissed her.

"Love's first kiss." I wonder what that will be like. What was it like the first time you and Alice kissed? Was it magical?

I spent the morning kissing my hand. Not that I am in love with it or anything, it was just practice. If and when the day should ever come that I kiss a boy, I want to be ready.

I've kissed magazines before, especially photos of hunky Chris Hartinger from *The Surfers of Solana Beach*. But magazines aren't like a real person. I considered taping a photo of one of the Solana Beach surfers on my hand, but then that would just be kissing a magazine all over again. So instead, I drew Prince Charming.

I made a fist with my left hand by tucking my thumb under my fingers. Then I drew two eyes and eyebrows. Now I know Prince Charming's head is a lot bigger than my hand, but still, it was a tiny bit like kissing a prince. Well, kissing him if he had a really small head, googly eyes, and a unibrow, and his mouth looked weird.

It felt exactly like . . . like I was kissing my hand. I wonder what a real kiss is like? I imagine that your heart starts to race, and your knees go weak, and you feel like you're floating. Is that how it was the first time you and Alice kissed?

Got your postcard from Motel 3 yesterday. Free coffee in the lobby, that's pretty neat! First I put your postcard on my bookshelf, then I moved it to my big mirror. Did I ever tell you that I like the way you write your name? You must be getting a lot of practice signing autographs!

I put a sticker on Lexington, and also Charleston, since I figured you'd go there next. Are you looking forward to Raleigh? My map is starting to fill up! When you go on your national tour, it will be fun to put stickers all over the whole country. After I put your latest postcard up, I reached for Elmo and panicked when the tape recorder didn't work. I couldn't believe I had lost my "Emily Song"!

"The Emily Song" was the one thing that made me feel like you were close. And now it's gone. I feel awful. Now there's no way I can hear you unless, of course, you call.

Emily

AUGUST 6

Dear Dad,

I was totally bummed about losing "The Emily Song," so I went to The Bookie to get some magazines to cheer myself up. But then I saw this one article about an abandoned dog that made me even more depressed. So I bought some treats for Mrs. Neederman's poodles with my credit card, plus I got them the most adorable sailor outfits. Mrs. Neederman hugged me when I gave them to her.

I get sad just thinking about pets or people being sad. That's why I have such a hard time at animal movies. Because if there's an animal starring in it, you can bet the dog will die, or the horse won't be able to race, or the mouse will be misunderstood. When I told this to Millie, she said, "I don't like to get sad."

"Sometimes we don't have a choice," I said.

"Emily, time to get off the phone!" Alice called out.

"Millicent, I have to go. Alice is forcing me to go on Neighborhood Watch again. Urgggg!!!!"

"Let's go, Emily! We're going to be late." Alice was standing by the front door shouting.

Late to what? Catching criminals? I mean, what would we do if we saw someone committing a crime? Both start screaming and run away? One of the reasons we moved here, she said, was because it was so safe. It certainly isn't safe from crazy mothers.

"What was it like the first time you saw Dad?" I asked as we headed out. "Was it love at first sight?"

I love thinking about the first time the two of you got together. It's one of the few things you agree on. I used to get so sick of the both of you telling your story, how you'd finish each other's sentences. Now I miss it.

Alice slowed down and turned off her flashlight. "I was writing my first big magazine article. *Rolling Stone* hired me to interview up-and-coming bands, and the Talky Boys were at the top of the list." She smiled. "Your father was this garage-band grunge guy with gorgeous eyes and long, flowing blond hair. I was so nervous. The funny thing was, later he told me that *he* was the one who was scared because a muckety-muck big-time reporter was going to interview him. But when I showed up, he was shocked at how young I was.

"We went out for coffee and talked through lunch and dinner, and at the end of the evening I just knew that he was the one for me. Of course, I was in serious journalist mode, so we didn't get involved until after I finished the article. By then I was totally smitten. Only I wasn't sure if he felt the same way. After all, I had mousy brown hair, and I wore preppy clothes, and I wasn't the groupie type. But the first time he kissed me, it felt so right. Like it was meant to be. . . ."

Two months after that, you two were married. How romantic is that?

Alice just stared off at the stars, and for the first time

since we got to Rancho Rosetta she looked relaxed. It wasn't until we had walked two blocks and she tripped on her long skirt that she remembered to turn her flashlight back on.

When did the two of you become strangers? What happened? Does it just go away after twenty years of marriage?

I don't ever want to stop feeling the way I do about Stanford Wong. When I think about him I feel all tingly inside. Wonderful thoughts take over and push away any bad feelings, and everything just seems right.

Ms. Martinez says that *Romeo and Juliet* has lots of complications. It's about "star-crossed lovers." I like the sound of that, even though I don't know what it means. Juliet, Ms. Martinez told me, was only thirteen years old. That's about my age. And to think, there was a famous play written about Juliet and her boyfriend. I still haven't read it, but I plan to.

If I were a better writer, I'd write a play called *Stanford and Emily*. Or maybe I'd make it into a musical and you could write the songs. Maybe Alice could help with the writing. It would just be the three of us working on a project. Wouldn't that be great? Think about it, okay? It would be totally professional, I promise.

Love,
Emily

AUGUST 7

Dear Daddy,

It's safe!!! "The Emily Song" is still here. The batteries were dead, that's all. Mr. Min figured it out.

When I got back from Millie's today, I scoured the house for quarters. I save them up, and when my Mongo Bongo cup is full, I feed the parking meters.

"Emily? Emily Ebers?" It was Officer Ramsey. "May I ask what you are doing?"

"Nothing."

"Oh, it's just that I thought I saw you putting money into that parking meter. I didn't know your mother rode a motorcycle."

"She drives a Prius," I informed Officer Ramsey. "You know, one of those hybrid, kind-to-the-environment cars."

"Well, that sounds more like the Alice I know."

What did he mean by that?

"Please tell her I said hello, and I hope to bump into her at Stout's again soon. Let her know that next time the coffee's on me." *Alice and Officer Ramsey had coffee together?* "Oh, and of course I hope you'll be there too."

"I don't drink coffee."

Officer Ramsey laughed. "Of course not! But maybe you can have a soda or a milk shake."

"I don't drink sodas or milk shakes."

"Oh. What about lemonade? Maybe you could have a lemonade?"

"I don't like lemonade."

"I see. Well, maybe it was not a great idea." He shook his head. "Sorry. Bad idea. Right. Okay, well, I'll see you around town."

Millie was tying her shoes in the gym. She has a special way she loops the laces and claims she's going to patent it. When she saw me, she leaped up and grinned. "Another day, another volleyball game."

"Alice and Officer Ramsey had coffee together."

"Wow, alert the press."

"Do you think he's hitting on her?"

"If having coffee with someone means he's hitting on her, then that means he also hits on Maddie. She has coffee with him all the time. They've been friends ever since he arrested her for putting Greenpeace stickers on SUVs."

Before I could say another word, Julie aimed a ball at us. "Heads up!" she shouted. As the ball came speeding toward us, Millie threw herself at it and did the most incredible dig.

"Good work, Millicent!" Coach Gowin cried. "See, when you use your whole body and not just your head, you get better results."

Midway through our game, Stanford showed up and I was so flustered that I missed an easy block. Julie nudged one of her backup singers and then waved to him. He waved back. I cringed, even though he waved to me and Millie first.

"Shall we get ice cream?" I asked Millicent after the game was over. Stanford was no longer in the bleachers. I wasn't sure where he had gone. I hoped he wasn't with Julie.

"No, I promised Maddie I'd catalog her postcard collection," Millie answered. "But have a cone for me, okay? Chunk o' Chocolate or something. You know what I like."

So there I was, standing in line and wondering if I really should have two ice-cream cones, when the door opened. I looked up and my eyes locked with his!!! It was Stanford Wong — in person. I tried not to faint as I attempted to stand upright and breathe at the same time. I couldn't stop smiling, and then I remembered my crooked front tooth and what Dr. Jill said about braces. So I tried not to smile, but failed.

"Hi Stanford! Can I buy you an ice cream?"

Did my voice sound squeaky? Was I being too forward? Was it okay that I offered to pay? Alice always paid for everything and you never seemed to mind.

Stanford looked surprised, then happy. "Hey, thanks. That would be nice, er, I mean cool. Whatever."

I exhaled.

"Stanford." It felt so great to say his name. Stanford. *Stanford and Emily. Emily and Stanford. Stanford and Emily.* Stanford. "STANFORD!" I heard myself say.

"Huh? What's wrong?"

"Oops. Nothing. I was just wondering what flavor you'd like?"

It was nearly impossible for me to take my eyes off of him and look up at the flavor board, but I forced myself to. I was afraid that if I looked at Stanford I'd start babbling again, or that I wouldn't be able to stop repeating his name. *Stanford, Stanford, Stanford, Stanford. Stanford and Emily. Stanford.*

S-T-A-N-F-O-R-D.

"Uh, what are you having?"

I hesitated. What if I ordered a flavor that he thought was weird? Or worse, what if I picked something he hated? I was trying to decide when Stanford suddenly whacked me on the shoulder.

"Stanford?"

"A bug?" he said. "You had a bug on you."

"Oh! Ewww. Thank you, Stanford. Was it a big one?"

"What?"

"The bug."

"Oh, the bug. Yeah, it was huge."

"I'm so glad you got it." I really was. "I hate bugs."

Stanford Wong is my hero.

"I think I'm going to try chocolate peanut butter," I told him.

"That's exactly what I was going to get!"

See, we are meant for each other.

As I paid for the cones, I could see Stanford gawking at my credit card. "My dad gave it to me," I said proudly. He was totally impressed.

After we got our ice cream, Stanford suggested we go outside to the benches. Millie wouldn't have sat down because of the bird poop, but Stanford sat on the poop side so I could have the clean part. What was it that Mrs. Buono always said? "Chivalry is dead." Not in Rancho Rosetta!

For a while it was sort of awkward with both of us just focusing on our ice-cream cones. I tried to think of fascinating things to say, but my mind kept going blank. Fortunately Stanford spoke up.

"Emily, I just read a great book and thought maybe you'd like to have it."

"Really? Wow!" Stanford Wong was giving me something! "You must read a lot of books, so I am sure it's a good one."

"Oh, it is," he said confidently. He reached into his back pocket, pulled out a paperback, and handed it to me.

"*The Outsiders*," I said, reading the title. I wasn't sure if he was giving it to me, or loaning it to me, so I said, "I'll be sure to get it back to you after I'm done."

"No, no, it's for you to keep. Look, I've signed it on the inside."

I handed him my cone so I could open the book. There were basketballs doodled all over the title page. Near the bottom it read:

> To Emily,
> I hope you enjoy this super terrific book.
> Sincerely yours,
> Your friend,
> Stanford A. Wong

I was disappointed it didn't say, "Love, Stanford," but still, he gave me a book. His favorite book. To keep! *The Outsiders*. I wondered if it's about nature? I love nature. I wished I had something to give to him but the only things I had in my purse were Lip Smackers, my credit card, a couple of quarters, and a plastic giraffe I got from a gumball machine.

As I was rereading the inscription (Maddie was right about his penmanship), Stanford asked me not to tell Millie about the book. He's afraid she might feel funny since she's so bad at English.

"Well," I told him, "I certainly don't want Millie to feel bad. All right, I won't mention it to her."

He looked relieved.

Isn't Stanford Wong just the most thoughtful boy you've ever heard of? You can totally tell he'd never do anything to hurt anyone. Just thinking about him makes me happy.

Love,
Emily

AUGUST 8

Hi Dad,

Want to hear something weird about Millie? This afternoon I was at Shah's and had just paid for some earrings with my credit card when someone tapped me on the shoulder.

"Hi, Wendy, what's up?"

"Not much."

"I have to meet my mom in half an hour."

"Do you want to hang around until then?" I asked.

"Sure, that'll be fun," she said. "Where's Millicent?"

"Probably at her grandmother's or someplace."

"Are you two best friends?"

I nodded.

"Too bad you won't be going to the same school."

"Oh, I know! I wish she wasn't homeschooled."

"Homeschooled?" Wendy looked surprised. "I thought Millicent was in high school and she's really, really smart, like freaky genius smart."

I had to laugh. Millie a genius? I almost told Wendy that she can't even make it through English without Stanford Wong, but then that would have embarrassed Millie. So instead I just smiled and said, "Hmm... interesting."

I'm not going to tell Millie what Wendy said. It's just way too random. Plus, I don't want to make Millie feel even worse about needing a tutor.

Wendy and I wandered around the mall, and I helped her pick out a new top, a burnt orange cami with lace trim. "This will look good if you layer it," I said. "Or maybe add a pin near the shoulder."

"You really know fashion," Wendy gushed. "Even Julie thinks so."

"Julie told you that?"

Wendy took her bag from the Tavares Teens salesgirl. "Not exactly, but I did hear her tell that to Alyssa. And Julie's known as the fashion queen at school, so for her to say that is a real compliment."

Julie talks about me and says nice things?

Wendy and I said our good-byes when her mom showed up, and then I headed home. Alice picked up Italian takeout for dinner. As we were in the kitchen putting the penne on plates, she got some pesto sauce on her tie-dyed top. It sort of just blended in with the pattern. Alice didn't notice, and I didn't say anything. I'll bet Alice is the only person who has ever ironed a tie-dye top. Hey, maybe she'll win another award: Most Uptight Hippie.

When she first started this hippie business she claimed she was "going with the flow, determined to be less uptight, more loose." But the only thing loose about her is the ridiculous clothes she insists on wearing.

I noticed she had pierced her ears again. When we moved here she wore clip-ons. Now she has a total of five holes in her ears. I'm afraid she's going to get her nose pierced, or worse, get a tattoo. Not that there's anything wrong with tattoos. Libby has a tattoo, and I really love your Talky Boys one, even if you did have to wear long-sleeved shirts when you sold houses.

Thankfully, it was just Millie who had come to dinner. Nicole or A.J. would have said something about Alice's top for sure. But Millicent isn't that into clothes, no matter how much I hint that she could be slightly more fashion-forward. It doesn't make sense. She's already got the trendy faux briefcase and nailed the stark look in her room. I've even clipped pages in my magazines with examples of outfits she would look fabulous in. But she always just wears jeans and T-shirts with funny sayings on them. Last week she wore the exact same thing three days in a row.

"Hey, Millie, have you ever seen *Marieke's Makeover Madness*?" I asked as we sat down to dinner.

"Is that the show where they rebuild ancient ruins in forty-eight hours?"

"No, it's where they make over how you look and dress and even walk and act and everything. It's a great show."

"Why would anyone submit themselves to something like that? How degrading."

"I dunno, it might be fun." I hesitated. "So, I guess that means you won't let me do a makeover on you?"

"Dream on, Emily Ebers."

Alice handed me the garlic bread. "Pass this to Millie, I know how much she likes it." She turned to Millicent.

"So how is your summer school class going? Do you feel you're learning a lot?"

"Everything's just great," Millie said. Usually it doesn't seem to bother her that Alice bombards her with questions. But this time she got sarcastic, and I tried not to snicker when she said, "With each class I find myself gaining a greater critical and aesthetic understanding of poetry and its importance to our society."

"That's pretty impressive for a middle school student," Alice remarked as she picked up her glass of iced tea. "I'd love to talk to you and your father someday about homeschooling. It's such a big trend, maybe I can do an article and you two can be in it."

Millie gulped. "My dad's shy."

"He is not," I chipped in. That was like saying Maddie acts like an old lady.

"I find it interesting that you go to summer school to supplement your homeschooling." Alice would just not drop the subject. Was I the only one who could see that Millie was clearly embarrassed? "Is it odd being the sole student in one venue and then being in a classroom full of kids for another?"

"Uh, no."

"Emily mentioned that you have a tutor."

"Mommmm . . ." I started to say, then caught myself. "Alice, really!"

"That's all right. Having a tutor is nothing to be ashamed of, is it, Millicent?" Before Millie even had a chance to answer, she went on. "It's great that your father recognizes he needs assistance teaching English, and to have that boy, what is his name . . . ?"

"Stanford," Millie and I muttered at the same time.

"Yes, for that Stanford boy to tutor you is so thoughtful of him. He must be a very nice and smart young man."

"Oh! He's supersmart," I couldn't help but tell her. "He knows everything about books. If it weren't for him, Millie would probably fail her summer school class."

Millie looked like she was dying. "Well, it's true," I told her. "But don't worry, Stanford won't let you fail. He told me that if you'd just stop goofing around and start taking your studies seriously, you'll do fine."

"You two talk about me? When?"

I blushed. "We've bumped into each other a couple times around town."

"I'd love to meet him someday," Alice noted as she sprinkled more cheese on her penne.

Panic! Total and complete panic. I looked over at Millie and we both pushed our plates away and stood up at the same time.

"Great dinner, Alice," she said.

"Yes, but we're done," I added.

"But you both hardly ate anything. What about dessert? I bought a Snickers cheesecake. . . ."

We were locked in my room before she could even finish her sentence.

"Phew, that was close," Millie said.

"Yeah, Alice is the last person I want to discuss Stanford with. But speaking of Stanford — "

"Ohhhh nooooo . . . Stanford this. Stanford that," Millie started singing. "Stanford this. Stanford that. Ooooh, Stanford! Stanford, Stanford, Stanford, you are soooooooo cute . . . Stanford!"

I threw a pillow at her and hit her right smack in the head. Volleyball has improved my aim immensely.

After Millie went home I reread the inscription Stanford wrote in the book. I have it memorized, but still I look at it all the time. I've started reading *The Outsiders*, and it's not about camping or anything outdoors. So far, it's about dead parents and gangs and fighting. I wonder what Stanford is trying to tell me? What is he thinking? What do boys think about? Does Stanford ever think about me, I wonder? Do you?

BTW, do you notice anything different? I'm using a fountain pen! I bought it at this fancy stationery store on Fair Oaks Avenue called Stahl Miller. It was a little pricey, but I figured that was okay because it's for both of us. Me to write with, and you to read what I write!

Love,
Emily

AUGUST 9

Dad,

I got the strangest letter today from A.J. At first I was happy, but when I began reading, she started saying all these insane things, like that her sister Celina saw you with some lady and a girl about my age at Radio City in New York!

"Maybe it wasn't really him. Maybe she just saw someone who looked like him," Millicent reasoned.

I was lying on the floor in the Mins' living room, clutching a pillow. Millicent was watching the news and taking notes. I thought Alice was the only one who did that.

"Or maybe your dad is dating some gold digger, and he's not the person you think he is," Millie added.

I stopped punching the pillow long enough to glare at her. "Of course he is who I think he is. He's my dad and he would never lie to me!"

"Okay, sorry." An RV commercial came on and Millie muted the television.

"I really think A.J.'s sister was mistaken, like you first said," I told her. "I mean, Celina always gets the surfers of Solana Beach mixed up, and she hardly knows my dad. A lot of men are balding and have goatees. And anyway, how could he be in New York City when he's on the road with the Talky Boys?"

"True," Millie quickly agreed. "It probably was just a case of mistaken identity."

"Yeah, that's it. A mistake. I just know my dad would never even think of taking someone else to Radio City Music Hall. Oh, Millie," I sighed, "sometimes I wish I had never come to Rancho Rosetta."

Millicent closed her notebook and clipped her pen onto the front of it. "Well, there is one good thing about you coming to Rancho Rosetta."

"And that would be . . . ?"

"Me! We wouldn't be best friends if you never came here."

It was true. I would never have met Millicent or the Mins, or Maddie, or Libby, or Stanford, Stanford, Stanford Wong.

Millie had an odd look on her face. I hoped I hadn't hurt her feelings. "Millicent Min, we're best friends forever! I like that we can tell each other everything and not have to worry about what the other person thinks," I assured her. "Like that Stanford is tutoring you. You were honest enough to own up to it, even though I know that was hard for you. I can't tell you how much I admire you for that.

"I feel like you're the only person I can be totally honest with. If I try to tell Alice about how I feel about Dad, she gets all weirded out and cries. Millie, you're the only person I can totally trust."

Millicent looked embarrassed, but then some people

are funny and can't take compliments. I am so glad Millie and I have each other. If you can't confide in your best friend, who can you confide in? I mean, Mrs. Buono always used to say, "Honesty is the best policy," right?

So, um, about Celina saying that she saw you with a lady and a girl at Radio City? Not that it really happened, but say, if it did, what was that all about? Who was that lady? That girl? Why were you at Radio City when you're supposed to be on the road?

I can't imagine that you'd go to Radio City with someone else. You didn't, did you? Tell me you didn't. Tell me it isn't true. It just can't be, can it?

Emily

AUGUST 10

Dearest Daddy,

First, I'm sorry if I got so spazzed out in my last entry. I've been thinking it over and feel pretty dumb. It's just that things are a little weird for me right now. Sometimes I feel like we're just here for vacation and will be back in Allendale in time for school to start. Other times I feel like New Jersey was lifetimes away and I'll never see it again. Sometimes I'm even scared I'll never see *you* again.

So sorry about my weirdness. Celina was just confused, I'm sure of it. She's always been a little spacey. After I wrote in my letter journal yesterday, I headed to Zooi's Zowie Music-teria, and you'll never guess what I bought. A guitar! I know, I know, I don't play the guitar—well, not yet anyway. Mr. Zooi teaches guitar and I might take lessons, or you can teach me. In the meantime, I've got this cool guitar, even if it doesn't have any strings and is kind of battered. There are stickers all over the back. I wonder who used to own it. Was it someone who had their own band? Someone famous, possibly?

Things really turned around for me today. Are you ready for my good news? Stanford Wong called! He asked Millie and me to meet him at the mall.

"We'd love to!" I told Stanford. I tried not to laugh as Millie hit herself over the head with a magazine.

He was waiting for us in front of the sporting goods store when we arrived. "Hi Emily!" he called out. "Hello, Millicent."

We had the best time. I kept hoping we'd bump into Julie, or at least one of her backup singers who would tell her they saw me with Stanford Wong. He ate three slices of pizza by stacking them on top of each other. I had one slice, and Millie said she wasn't hungry. Afterward, we got all goofy playing Millicent's Would You Rather game.

Stanford asked, "Would you rather fart really loud in an elevator full of your teachers, or in an elevator full of high school kids?"

I said teachers and Millie said students. Then it was my turn.

"Would you rather be in an ad for underwear or be in an ad for diarrhea medicine?"

"Do you actually have to take the medicine?" Stanford asked.

"No. But in the ad you have to look like you're taking it and smile."

"Can the underwear be really old-fashioned, like in the eighteen-hundreds when they wore those knickers that covered up everything?" Millie gets really serious when we play this.

"Nope, it would be whatever underwear you're wearing now."

"Then I'd go for diarrhea," Millicent announced.

"Yeah, me too," Stanford agreed. "At least with that you could say you were acting."

"You just said that because your underwear is probably dirty!" Millie said, laughing.

"Is not," Stanford shouted back. "Unlike yours!"

We all cracked up. It's like I have two best friends again. Only one's a boy who makes my heart want to sing.

As we turned to enter the bookstore, Stanford and I bumped into each other. I pretended not to notice, but my heart began to race and I couldn't blink for the longest time. Millie and I took our time choosing Archie comics. We got different ones so we could swap when we're done. She didn't want Stanford to know she reads comics, probably because he'd tell her she ought to be reading more books. So I bought the Archie for her while she pretended to be interested in the history section of the bookstore.

Later, the three of us took pictures in the photo booth. It was fun cramming together, and at one point I had to sit on Stanford's lap. Then right before the flash, he shoved Millie out of the booth.

"Hey!" she yelled when she hit the floor.

"Stanford," I scolded. "That wasn't very nice."

"Oops. Sorry, Millicent," he said, not sounding very sorry.

Don't ever tell Millie this, but I was glad she wasn't in the picture. I love having a photo of just Stanford and me together. Can you wear something out by staring at it?

Happily yours,

Emily

AUGUST 11

To Whom It May Concern,

I had been so happy that I felt guilty thinking about you all alone on the road with the Talky Boys. Plus, I felt awful that I believed Celina even for a second. Then I had this totally brilliant idea: I would leave a surprise message on your answering machine. That way, every time you called in — if you ever called in — you could hear me.

Even though it was almost midnight here, and 3 a.m. in New Jersey, I knew it wouldn't matter what time it was since you weren't home. So with the $1.34 left on my phone card, I dialed.

The phone rang three times.

"Hello?" The woman sounded like she had been asleep.

"Oh, I am sooo sorry. Wrong number."

"Okay," she said before hanging up.

How embarrassing was that?

I called again, this time making sure I was dialing the right number.

"Hello?" the same lady said.

"Hello?"

"Who is this?" she asked.

I was so confused.

"Is this David Ebers's house?"

"Yes, it is. Who are you?"

"Is he there?"

"Who is this?"

"Peggy, who is it?" I heard you say.

"Prank call," she said before the phone went dead.

I couldn't breathe. You're home? You're not on the road? Is that why I haven't gotten any postcards lately? Who was that lady? Why didn't you tell me you were back? How come you never told me? Who was that lady?

I couldn't call you because I didn't know where you were. But you knew where I was. I've been right here the whole time. You could have called me anytime. Who was that lady? Who are you? You're not my dad, my dad would have told me he was home.

Emily

AUGUST 12

Dear Father,

Today I stayed in my room all morning. Each time the phone rang, I hoped it would be you. I told Millie I had to keep the line open since I was expecting a call.

"Don't you have call-waiting?"

"Yes, but I don't want to take any chances."

"Did you tell him to call you back?"

"No."

"Then why would he?"

"He just will, I know it."

"Emily, he's called exactly once this entire summer. Odds are he's not going to call this morning."

"Whatever. Listen, Millie, I have to get off the phone."

"But Maddie's getting her passport photo taken and she said we could come make faces at her. If we can get her to crack up, she'll buy us the Bottomless Bucket o' Popcorn at the Rialto."

It was tempting, but I had to decline. I clutched my friendship necklace and stared at the phone.

At lunchtime, Millicent came over and forced me to get out of the house. "You've got to eat sometime," she said. Sometimes I'm glad she's so bossy.

I made sure the answering machine was working before we left. The day got a thousand times better when we ran into Stanford at Mel's and the three of us ended up walking near the train tracks. We were talking about cliques and I said, "I don't think people should pretend to be something they're not." And all of a sudden Stanford got all serious and said, "Emily, you are so solid."

I gasped. Stanford had never been mean before.

"He thinks I'm fat," I whispered to Millie.

Instantly, she turned around and kicked Stanford really hard and then smacked him on the head with what looked like one of Maddie's kung fu moves.

"Hey!" he yelled, hopping up and down on one leg.

"Emily's not fat, you stupid, inconsequential pile of beetle dung! We hate you!" Millicent shouted before kicking his other leg.

"What?! I never said she was *fat*, I said she was *solid*. You know, not flaky like *some* girls," he said, glaring at Millie. "I can't stand flaky girls. Solid's a good thing!"

"Oh. Then never mind," Millicent said as she calmly picked up her briefcase and continued walking.

As bad as I felt for Stanford, who was still limping, it felt wonderful that Millicent would stick up for me like that. She really is a true friend.

So Stanford thinks I'm solid, and that solid is a good thing. Still, I wonder, does he think I'm fat? I wonder if I weigh more than him?

After the three of us parted, I headed down Fair Oaks Avenue to Stahl Miller. I bought boxes of stationery, pads of paper, and colorful envelopes. I even splurged on a whole set of fancy pens.

"Are all these for you?" Mr. Miller asked as I handed him my credit card.

"No, they're for my dad," I said as I signed the receipt.

"He must love to write letters."

I just nodded.

When I got home I spread the stationery out all over my bed. I had bought more than I realized.

I stared at my phone for a while, then before I could chicken out, I dialed really fast.

"Hello?" It was that same lady. "Hello? Elise, is that you?"

I hung up.

Maybe that lady is your cousin? Do you even have a cousin?

I'm waiting for you to tell me the phone call was all a silly misunderstanding. There's got to be a logical answer for what happened last night. Like, maybe that lady was one of the Talky Boys' wives, and for some reason you had a big sleepover at your apartment. Or maybe you just got back from the road last night and that was some woman who was delivering pizza, and you were going to call me but were afraid it was too late.

Or, maybe, maybe you were home to get your things and that lady was helping you, and you're going to call me and say, "Emily, I'm coming to Rancho Rosetta!" Or maybe you're just going to show up and surprise me!

Well, whatever the reason is, I'm sure it's a good one. I can't wait to get this whole silly mess cleared up.

Sincerely,
Emily

AUGUST 13

Dear Person Who Is So Not a Part of My Life,
Last night I slept over at Millie's again. At breakfast, Mrs. Min said, "Millicent, I'm going to the office now. Before I get home, I'd like you to get the good place mats out of the armoire. Please have it done before dinner."

Millie was busy making words out of her Alphabets cereal, so I thought I'd help out. I always like to help Mrs. Min whenever I can.

It took a couple tries to get the armoire open. Finally

I tugged hard on the handle and a bunch of stuff tumbled out. I was scared that something might have broken, so I quickly began picking all the things up and putting them on the dining room table. They looked like awards, probably belonging to Millie's parents, I thought.

I was wrong.

"Emily, everything okay?" Millicent called out.

I didn't answer. I couldn't answer. I was in shock. A Quiz Bowl Champion silver cup? A First Place Math-a-lete trophy? A *Junior Jeopardy!* Grand Champion plaque? They were all engraved with Millicent's name.

Slowly, then faster and faster, I started piling awards on the table. A Rancho Rosetta Middle School diploma, more certificates, chess trophies, debate trophies, Cryptarithm trophies. *What the heck is a Cryptarithm?* Plaques, newspaper articles, a framed photo of a young Millie on *The Tonight Show with Jay Leno*. These were all Millie's! But why? It didn't make sense.

Millie walked into the room. Before she could say anything, I asked, "What does this mean, Millicent? Are these all yours?" Her face turned pale. "Tell me," I said as I gripped a framed article with the headline "Child Prodigy Enters High School at Age 9."

"You were snooping!" Millie cried.

"I was not. I was getting the place mats and I found these! Are all of these yours? They have your name on them."

Then I remembered what Wendy had said about Millicent being a genius. Duh! Suddenly everything made sense. Why Millie was so secretive, why Millie was vague about school, why Millie sometimes used big words and said things no one could understand.

"How could you do this to me?" I yelled. "I heard rumors, but I didn't believe them. We're never going to be in the same grade, you don't even go to middle school anymore. You're a genius, a stupid genius!"

She just stood there staring, like there was something seriously wrong with me.

"When were you going to tell me? Are you even listening to me? Millicent???!!! What's the matter with you? Why are you just standing there? Aren't you going to say anything?"

"Intelligence," she began slowly, "merely refers to the all-around effectiveness of an individual's mental processes. . . ."

"Don't you get it? Millicent, what is your problem?" She just looked at me blankly. "It's not about how smart you are, it's that you didn't tell me! Didn't you think I'd find out? Didn't you think it would hurt my feelings to be the last to know? Didn't you trust me? Didn't you think at all? And why then, if you're supposed to be so smart, do you even need a tutor? Why does Stanford have to tutor you . . ."

Then it hit me. Of course. I'd been so stupid. "You

lied about that too, didn't you? Stanford's not tutoring you, you're tutoring him. Geez, Millicent, you're really something. I can't believe I thought you were my friend. Best friends don't lie to each other."

I grabbed my overnight bag and ran out the front door. I hoped Millicent would try to stop me, but she didn't.

As I marched through Rancho Rosetta I could barely see where I was going. My eyes kept filling with tears. I could not believe it. Millicent Min. A genius? And Stanford. Stanford Wong lied to me too. They both lied. I thought Millie was my best friend, and I really, totally trusted Stanford. I thought he was different from other boys. I thought he actually *like* liked me. What kind of a sick joke were they —

Boom! I bumped into someone and fell to the ground.

"Emily, is everything all right? You don't look so good."

Officer Ramsey helped me up and handed me my overnight bag. "I'm fine. Everything's great. Just fine."

"Okay." He hesitated. "Just checking. Would you like a ride home?"

"I'm fine, really, I'm fine," I said, wiping the tears from my face.

"All right then, take care. Give my best to your mother."

By the time I reached home, I felt like throwing up. Alice was sitting on the floor going through boxes.

"Emily! You're home early." She looked me up and

down. "You might want to change out of your monkey pajamas."

I was breathing hard and trying not to cry.

"Honey? Is anything wrong?"

Alice rose and started toward me with her arms outstretched. I needed a hug, but I willed her to stop. "I'm fine. I was just, um, I was . . . jogging."

"Jogging? In your slippers?"

"That's what I said, isn't it? You don't believe me?"

"Okay. Okay. You were jogging." Alice took a deep breath and pasted on a smile. "Well, they found the missing boxes! Emily, look at this photo of us. It's from that summer we vacationed in Vancouver, when you were in second grade. . . ."

With every stupid thing Alice kept saying, I felt myself getting more and more tense. Finally she stopped talking and looked at me. "Are you sure you're okay? Emily, please, talk to me. What's the matter?"

"STOP ASKING ME SO MANY QUESTIONS!"

"Okay, Emily," she said softly. "I'm just worried about you."

"Well, if you were so worried about me, then why did you make us move here and leave everyone and everything behind? Why didn't you ask me what I thought about anything? Instead, you just did what you wanted to do and didn't even think about me!"

With every step Alice took toward me, I took a step backward.

"Emily . . ."

"Leave me alone!"

I slammed the door to my room, only it wasn't my room. My room was back in our house in Allendale, waiting to be demolished. I took down your postcards and ripped them up. I shredded the quizzes Millicent Min and I did together, and when I got to the photos of Stanford and me, I stopped cold.

I dumped my Stanford Wong box onto the floor, took out his Zappo Zit, and flushed it down the toilet. It whirled around before going down and coming back up again. No matter how many times I flushed it, I could not get rid of it. Finally I fished the tube out and tossed it into the sink.

Stanford lied to me. This whole summer he and Millicent were playing some sort of stupid joke on me. A.J. and Nicole are probably laughing at me too. They've only sent me two letters this entire summer. And you. Do you and Alice have any idea what you are doing to me?

Do you want to know the best day of my life, and the worst day? Well, it was the same day. You and Alice got all dressed up and so did I. You took me to Blum's Bistro and were acting nice to each other, something I hadn't seen in a long time. We looked like a happy family. I thought we were a happy family. Then right before dessert came you said that you and Alice had some big news.

Alice smiled and nodded without saying anything. I was so happy. I thought you guys were going to tell me

I was getting a sister or a brother, or at least a dog. Only, when it came time to tell me, you couldn't talk. Instead you got up and left the table. So Alice spoke and said that you were moving out again, and that this time it was permanent because the two of you were getting a divorce. And then the dessert came and none of us could eat it, and it was chocolate.

The ride home in the car was excruciating. Silent, except for the sound of Alice trying to muffle her sobs. Even when you turned the radio up really high, it couldn't mask the silence. Alice had lied to me. You had too. You both knew about the divorce coming, yet you acted like everything was fine. Not saying anything is the same as lying. Sometimes it's worse.

You are still silent. I should have expected that. Even when we lived in the same town, the only time we ever got together or talked was when I called you.

I've been thinking about this a lot, and if you truly loved me, you'd call. I'm waiting.

Emily L. Ebers

AUGUST 14

Dad,

Lavender's on the radio. She doesn't play your kind of music, but I like her. Lavender cares about people, unlike others I know.

I wandered around the mall this morning and bought so much stuff I thought the credit card would wear out. By the time I was done, I had so many shopping bags that I could barely carry them all home.

I called you in the afternoon, but hung up after one ring. Today at 2 p.m., Alice and I both cried in our bathrooms. It sounded like stereo, only she stopped first. She's not crying as long as she used to, but I've picked up the slack.

Sometimes when I cry I stare at my face in the mirror. When I first stare at myself it looks like me. Then after a while, if I stare hard without blinking, my face begins to morph and I look like someone else entirely. It's weird and scary and mesmerizing, and kind of cool in a strange way. Only when I stop crying, nothing's changed.

Sometimes I wish I were someone else completely. That I could just start over.

It's nighttime.

Alice keeps trying to talk to me through the door.

"Emily? Emily, I'm worried about you."

"I'm fine. Just leave me alone."

"Okay. Well, I'm leaving some food for you out here. You have to eat."

I waited until I was sure she was gone. The pizza tasted great and I devoured the grapes.

"Hello, you night owls out there." I turned the radio up. "You're listening to Lavender on this moonlit evening. And for all you lovers and lonely hearts, here's a special song just for you. . . ."

Lavender always knows exactly what to play. I could listen to her forever. You can just tell that she's been heartbroken, but she doesn't talk about herself. Instead she listens to what people tell her, and then tries to give them hope. When I grow up, I'm going to be like Lavender.

"Rachel," Lavender said gently, "you say that after three years of dating, he just stopped calling?"

"Yes," Rachel sobbed. "No warning, no nothing."

"Gee, that's got to be hard. Here's a little song that may help mend your broken heart. . . ."

Then she played "How Can You Mend a Broken Heart," by the Bee Gees. Have you ever heard of them? I can't tell if they are men or women singing.

Lately, it feels like everything is all jumbled up, like on that game show where you have to guess what the letters spell. Maybe Stanford and Millicent never liked me. Maybe you never loved me. I don't know who I can trust anymore. I looked around at all the stuff I bought today. Hats and vases and mugs and coffee beans and tons of CDs. But they didn't make me feel any better, so I just tossed everything in the closet. If I were on a game show, I'd be the big loser.

Emily

AUGUST 15

Dad,

I am really praying the phone whatever was just some sort of huge misunderstanding, but this waiting is getting harder and harder. Every day that passes makes me lose more hope. If I could just get one more postcard from the road, then I'd know it was all a silly mistake.

One thing I know I'm not mistaken about is this: Millicent Min and Stanford Wong lied to me. I tried to think of reasons to forgive them, but in the end I decided that they knew what they were doing was wrong, and they still went ahead with their lies. Did they think it wouldn't matter to me? Or that I'd just let it go?

At the library, Ms. Martinez greeted me warmly. I forced a smile, then hurried past her before she could ask me about *Romeo and Juliet*. I wasn't there to discuss books.

My former friends were sitting at a table in the back. I could hear them arguing before I could see them, but they both shut up instantly when they saw me.

"Stanford. Millicent," I said, delivering the speech I had

practiced. "I don't have much to say to either of you, other than I hope that you had fun with your little charade."

Stanford looked different. I couldn't tell how because I was afraid that if I looked directly at him, I'd fall apart. Instead, I tossed *The Outsiders* onto the table. "Here, you can have your book back. Even though you raved about it, I don't think I want to read it anymore."

I took my friendship necklace off and set it down next to the book. "I think this belongs to you," I told Millie. My voice began to crack. I had worn my necklace every day, even when it didn't match my outfit. "I hope the two of you have fun together making up lies. Good-bye."

Then, head held up high, I turned around and marched out of the library and straight to the mall, where the salespeople were happy to see me.

Lavender is on. She's playing a song called "That's What Friends Are For." Stevie Wonder is singing. He's blind, but you'd never know it by his songs. He sounds like he can see better than anyone.

When I gave Stanford and Millie their things back, the look of shock on their faces gave me a weird sort of satisfaction. It was as if I was in charge, if only for the moment. When I got home, I pulled your frying pan out from under my bed and put it in the kitchen. Now everything is where it's supposed to be.

I'm going to give TB extra hugs tonight. I really think he needs a friend right now.

Emily

AUGUST 16

Dad,

Alice said I had to go to volleyball, even though I had planned to go shopping. The last person I wanted to see was Millicent Min. I don't miss her at all. I don't miss the way she babbled on and on about boring subjects, and how when she got excited, she'd stand up and wave her arms around. I don't miss that she used to drag me to the Rialto to see those stupid black-and-white movies, although *Miracle on 34th Street* was pretty good. And I certainly don't miss how uptight she was about keeping her Archie comics alphabetized, even though it did make it easier to find certain issues.

I was at the gym warming up when I heard, "Hi Emily!"

"Millie?" I spun around. "Oh, hi Wendy."

"What's up?"

"Not much. What about with you?"

"We might get a Labradoodle puppy, but that probably won't happen. I think my dad just said he'd consider it so that my brother and I would stop bugging him."

"A dog would be nice. They're very loyal."

Coach Gowin blew her whistle. "Girls, line up!"

Millicent Min was usually in the front. Today she wasn't even at the back.

The game got off to a slow start and never picked up.

I made a ton of stupid mistakes. Julie didn't say anything, but I could tell she was upset. Maybe she was right when she insulted me that first day. Maybe I am fat, and that's why I'm so bad at volleyball. Maybe I'm just fat and ugly and that's why I don't have any friends. How could I even think that someone like Stanford Wong would ever want to be my boyfriend? How stupid was I to think that anyone would ever want me? You don't.

After the game, I went to the library. Millie and Stanford don't have tutoring on Fridays, but just in case they were there, I slipped *Romeo and Juliet* in the return box outside where I was sure not to bump into anyone. I didn't read it. I never finished *The Outsiders* either, so I don't know what happens. It probably has a really sad ending and everyone dies.

Emily

AUGUST 17

Dad,

Millicent has stopped coming to volleyball. I think I'm the only one who has noticed she's missing. Isn't it interesting how people can just disappear?

At today's game, Wendy scored three points in a row.

She's an excellent volleyball player. Even Julie thinks so. "Wendy, you should think about going out for the Rancho Rosetta team when school starts."

"Really? Oh, Julie, do you think I should?"

"Uh, I just said so, didn't I?"

Julie turned to me and I braced myself. "I liked the outfit you wore to the mall the other day. Wasn't it in *Gamma Girl*?"

"Yes," I stammered. Julie saw me at the mall and remembered what I was wearing, and now she was complimenting me? How weird was that?

As we rotated positions, I asked Wendy, "What are you doing after the game?"

"Nothing, really."

"Do you want to get a smoothie?"

"Sure!"

When it was my turn to serve, *bamm!* I hit the ball over the net.

I don't need Millicent Min or Stanford Wong. Or A. J. Schiffman or Nicole Kwan. Or even you or Alice. I can make new friends. I can make even better friends than the ones I had before.

At Smoothie Station, I ordered the Double Mocha Mango Delight.

"Those have a lot of calories," Wendy noted. "I'm having the Pineapple Passion, but made with all ice and no yogurt, and only half the pineapple and no orange juice."

Wendy talks about her weight a lot. She also talks about Julie a lot, which is weird, because Julie hardly notices Wendy.

"Julie's like *the* most popular girl at Rancho Rosetta. Last year she dated someone in high school. She's got the best clothes, and she has two cell phones, one for family and one for friends. Julie gets her hair highlighted, and her summer pedicure party is so exclusive that one girl who wasn't invited changed schools rather than face everyone."

"That'll be $6.94," the Smoothie Station guy said, handing us our drinks. Wendy's eyes lit up when I pulled out my credit card.

"No way!" she squealed. "It's got to be a fake! Is it a fake? It looks so real. Is it fake?"

"It's real," I said. "My dad gave it to me. Your drink's on me."

"Wow," Wendy said, taking a sip of her Pineapple Passion from a coffee stirrer. "Thank you. I've never even heard of someone our age having her own credit card! I'll bet you're the only kid in Rancho Rosetta with one."

"What are the kids around here like? Is it like volley-ball? You know, the popular ones and the rest of us."

Wendy stared deep into her smoothie, and I could tell she was giving my question some serious thought. "There are various levels of popularity," she finally said. "I'd rank Julie's group as A-plus. The Roadrunners are A-plus too — they're the basketball players. Then there are the rich kids, and the mean kids, and the geek kids, and the jocks, and the drama queens, the troublemakers, the brains, and the nobodies. You know, like any school."

I knew. Even though Wilcox Academy was small, we did have our cliques.

"What about you, Wendy? What group are you in?"

"Oh," she said, sounding disgusted. "I'm in with the regular girls. We're sort of in the middle. Not geeks, but not popular. Just average."

"What's wrong with that?"

"Nothing, except that we're considered boring and none of the cute guys will even look at us."

Wendy suddenly got quiet and began to chew on her coffee stirrer.

"Hey, we should exchange phone numbers," I said. "Maybe we can do more stuff together."

"That sounds good," she said, perking up.

"Want to go to the mall?" I asked.

"Oh, I'd love to, but I have to babysit my brother. Maybe some other time."

It felt good to see Wendy smile. But even though she's really nice and wants to be friends, I didn't feel as happy as I thought I should. I felt empty. What's the matter with me?

When I got home, I found a postcard waiting for me. At first I was really excited because I thought it was from you, but instead it was a reminder that my subscription to *Gamma Girl* is going to expire soon. I signed up for the five-year renewal option with my credit card. I also ordered a second *Gamma Girl* subscription to be sent to your house, in case I ever visit. While I was at it, I got a subscription to *Rolling Stone* for Alice and a subscription to *Senior Lifestyles* for you.

Emily

AUGUST 18

Dad,

Stanford called three times this afternoon, but he didn't say much. Actually, he didn't say anything. He just hung up when I answered. I knew it was him from the caller ID.

I'm so glad that I'm over him. I mean, all I did was think about him, day and night. Today I was constantly not thinking about him, which means that I had a lot of extra time. I was in my room not thinking about him, and then he called. Then I had to think about him, and then I forced myself not to. And then he called again. See what a pain he is? Maybe Millicent was right when she said, "He's not even worth a second thought."

I can't believe that I ever liked Stanford. Isn't it enough that he played a really mean trick on me? Now he's doing phone hang-ups. He's the one with the hang-ups. Like how stupid and immature he is. I guess I'm glad he never was my boyfriend. I wonder if Juliet had this much trouble with Romeo?

Wouldn't you know, today Alice asked me about the play?

"I returned it to the library."

She looked up from her fruit salad. "Really? Well, how did you like it?"

I considered lying, but there has been too much lying going on here already.

"I didn't read it."

"Oh," Alice said. I could see that she was pretending it was no big deal. "Well, that's okay, I guess. It was probably unfair of me to give you a reading assignment." She speared a grape with her fork. "You have much better things to do than hole up with a book!"

The sad fact was I didn't have anything better to do. Not anymore.

"I haven't seen Millie for a couple days," Alice continued. She offered me a strawberry, but I shook my head. "She must be busy with her studies. Why don't you invite her for a sleepover? I can order out for dinner. Millicent loves Pizza Wheels."

"I can't . . ."

"Sure you can, just call her."

"No, I mean, I can't. We're not talking."

Alice put down her fork. "Oh, honey, I'm sorry. Did you have a fight?"

"I guess you could say that."

"What happened?"

How could I explain to Alice what happened when I'm not sure myself? All I know is that Millicent didn't trust me enough to tell me the truth. That hurts more than whatever it was she was trying to hide from me.

"I don't want to talk about it."

Alice was quiet before saying, "Well, if you ever do want to talk. About Millicent, or anything, anything at all, I want you to know that I am here for you."

"Whatever."

"Emily, I am here for you, okay?"

"Yeah, okay. Now can I go?"

I've been using my BeDazzler a lot lately, but I can never seem to finish anything. Lavender is talking to a lot of sad people right now. I'm considering calling her. If I did, I'd tell her that I am all alone.

Wait . . . Lavender just said something amazing.

"Now for all the lonely people out there, I want to tell you, don't give up. There is hope over the horizon. Don't let sadness get the better of you. You can let loneliness beat you, or you can beat it. And you know that I'm in your corner, that's why this song is for you. . . ."

Now she's playing "Lonely People" by a band called America. Do you know them?

I am going to listen to Lavender now. She probably knows me better than anyone.

Emily

AUGUST 19

Dad,

Millie showed up for volleyball today. I ignored her, which was difficult since I was always glancing over to see if she was ignoring me. The whole time Julie kept making her usual snide remarks, not to Millie's face, but loud enough so everyone could hear.

"Oops! *Someone* really botched that last serve!"

"It helps to be awake when you play volleyball."

"What team is she on, ours or theirs?"

Julie made me so mad, but Millie made me madder. Why doesn't she defend herself?

After the game, Wendy and I headed out. I couldn't bear to look at Millicent as we left.

"Why did you stop hanging around with her?" Wendy asked. She was sipping her ever-present water bottle. Wendy says that drinking water all day tricks your stomach into thinking you're full.

"Oh, I don't know. It just wasn't, you know. We just didn't, I don't know."

"Is it that genius thing I told you about?" asked Wendy. "I've heard that she's really weird. Is she really weird? She seems nice, but definitely different."

"She's not weird! She's . . . quirky."

"Let's go this way," Wendy said, pulling my arm.

As we walked through the park, I could hear children playing. One little girl was stuck on the top of the slide. Below her, the other kids were yelling at her to come down, but she kept shaking her head as she gripped the rails.

"Look!" Wendy said reverently. "They're here."

Through the parted trees, I could see why Wendy was gawking. There on the basketball court was a group of five incredibly good-looking boys. I was riveted by the sight of them, and one in particular.

Stanford snuck the ball away from a red-headed boy. Then he leaped up like he was flying through the sky and made a basket. Three of the boys high-fived Stanford. One stood off to the side. I just stared.

"Those are the Roadrunners." Wendy whispered even though no one was near us. "*The* most popular boys in the whole school."

"Really?" I choked.

"You know Stanford Wong, don't you? We've all seen you talk to him after volleyball. He's the leader of the group. Couldn't you just die thinking about him?"

I was dying as Wendy spoke.

"Stanford is going to be on the A-Team when school starts. It's, like, historic. No seventh-grader has ever played basketball on the A-Team. Usually it's only eighth-graders. He's that good — and sooooo cute too. Well, I'm sure you already know that. How do you know him?"

"His family's friends with Millicent's family," I mumbled.

"Oh! That makes sense. Anyway, see the tall

Roadrunner? His name is Stretch. He's the one we both saw that day in the grocery store, remember?"

How could I forget? The movie-star boy was right in front of me. The one who handed me the Doritos.

"He's the strong silent type," Wendy was saying. "And I do mean that. It's said he hasn't talked for two years because his vocal cords got damaged when he saved toddler triplets from drowning. But who cares if he can talk or not? Just look at him, isn't he the dreamiest guy you've ever seen?"

Second dreamiest.

"Over there," Wendy went on, "the boy with all the really curly, dark brown hair, that's Gus. He gets in lots of trouble for all the pranks he plays — he once released white mice into the girls' locker room. But he's super-funny and can make anyone laugh — even the teachers can't stay mad at him. And the little guy, that's Tico. He's really nice and friendly. All the girls love Tico."

"What about that boy over there?" I pointed to the one with red hair. He had a scowl on his face.

"That's Digger Ronster. His dad owns Ronster's Monster RV World."

"The one with the commercials on television?"

"Yep, that's him. The Ronsters are really rich, and Digger likes to remind people about that. Digger's sort of scary. No one wants to get on his bad side."

We hid behind the trees and watched the Roadrunners play basketball. Sometimes Stanford made spectacular shots, other times he played just like the rest of the guys. Only, to me, he would never be just like anyone else. I miss Stanford. I miss you, too. How pathetic is it to miss people who don't even care you exist?

Emily

P.S. I'm still writing this to you because I'm still holding out a teeny-tiny sliver of hope that I misinterpreted the phone call. So if that's the case, then just ignore all the bad stuff I've written.

Oh! And I bought you another pen. This one's even better than the other ones. It's called a Montblanc, and Mr. Miller of Stahl Miller guaranteed me that whoever owns one of these will never want to stop writing.

AUGUST 21

Dad,

I wasn't expecting anything good to happen today, but something sort of did. After volleyball Wendy raced up to me and shouted, "We're in! We're in!"

"We're in what?"

She waved something in the air. "Look!"

Wendy was holding an invitation to Julie's pedicure party. Suddenly we were in with the popular girls.

"I don't get it. Why would she invite us? She hates us."

"Julie doesn't hate us, she's just very particular about who she has around her. But look!" As Wendy slid the invitation out of the envelope, some glitter fell to the floor. "We got invited. Do you know how hot invitations to her party are?"

"I don't think I want —"

"Oh please, please, please, you *have* to go. Please! Julie said, 'Wendy, you know Emily, right? Well, this is for both of you. Make sure Emily comes.'"

"She said that?"

Wendy gave me a huge hug. "Then it's settled! We'll go together. I'll pick you up at seven."

Alice and I got home at the same time.

"Where were you?" she asked.

"With Wendy. Where were you?"

Alice turned red. "Nowhere," she said. "Just out."

"I've been invited to a party at Julie's," I told her.

"I should probably talk to Julie's mother first," she said, reaching for the phone.

"Noooooooo!" I yelled. The last thing I needed was for Alice to embarrass me in front of Julie's mom and ruin my chances of making any new friends. "Uh, no. That's okay. Not a good idea. I mean, I've been playing volleyball with Julie all summer. I'm sure it's fine. Besides, Wendy's going with me."

"Will Millicent be there?"

"It's a really exclusive party. Wendy says only the most popular girls get invited to Julie's."

"Millicent's not popular?"

"Not exactly," I laughed. Instantly, I felt bad. When Alice didn't chide me, I felt even worse.

As I tried on dozens of outfits, the thought of going to the party started to cheer me up. Millie was never that interested in fashion or beauty, but Wendy is more like me. We've both had exactly one pedicure in our lives, and couldn't wait for number two.

"Come in, ladies." Julie's mom looked like she could be her sister. "Sodas are in the fridge, and the food is in the dining room." She glanced at me. "There's even celery and carrots if you're on a diet."

"Thank you!" Wendy said brightly.

"Gee, look, a carrot," I said as I grabbed one on our way to Julie's room. "Yum."

As we were led through the house, I looked around. There was a huge chandelier in the entrance hall and three couches in the living room. Wendy and I stuck close together.

"More guests," Julie's mom announced as she opened the door to Julie's room. There were a bunch of girls I had never seen before. Alyssa, Ariel, and Ariana were there too. Wendy calls them the Triple A's. One of them looked up when we came in.

"Hey, we're just picking polishes. Gigi should be here soon."

"Is Gigi one of your friends?" Wendy asked.

"Uh, noooo," Julie said. "Gigi's from the nail salon. Did you think we were going to sit around and give pedicures to each other?"

"We're not?" I asked.

The Triple A's burst out laughing. Wendy looked at them and then started laughing too. "Emily's such a crack-up. Always joking, aren't you, Emily?"

She nudged me in the ribs.

"Ouch! Oh. Yes, that's me. Emily the crack-up."

Wendy took me aside. "Emily, please try a little harder. These girls are the ones who can make or break you at school. See that one over there?" I looked at a gorgeous girl with dark hair and a perfect golden-bronze tan. She seemed familiar. "That's Betina. She's a model. She's been in *Gamma Girl* magazine! Isn't this exciting?"

I had to admit, it *was* exciting. Everyone looked like models with every hair in place. Millie mostly wore her hair in a ponytail using regular old rubber bands. And their clothes! Several girls were wearing outfits straight off the runway.

"Emily, is that a Henri G. skirt?" Julie asked.

I nodded.

"Now that," she announced to everyone in the room, "is a great skirt!"

I couldn't stop myself from grinning.

"Ohmygosh, what time is it?" Julie yelled as she

dove toward the channel changer. "We almost missed *Marieke's Makeover Madness*."

We gathered around the television just in time to watch the before and after of some girl from South Pasadena, who Marieke transformed from "Serious Samantha to Sensational Sammy!" Marieke can work miracles.

"Gigi's here!" Julie's mom called. "She's setting up in the living room."

"Come on," Julie ordered. "Let's go! I'll TiVo this."

As I was admiring the Red Rocket nail polish on my toes, Wendy remarked, "I just love *Marieke's Makeover Madness*. Imagine going from plain to pretty in one week!"

"Wait a minute," Julie said. "We can do that!"

"We can do what?" asked a Triple A.

"A makeover. We're fashion experts, aren't we? All we'd need is someone to make over."

The room got quiet. All heads turned in my direction. I turned around, too, but no one was behind me. A smile crept across Julie's face.

I gulped. "Uh, Wendy, can I talk to you for a moment?"

"Please, oh please," Wendy begged. We were huddled in the bathroom. "It will be so much fun! Plus if you let her make you over, we have it made at school. Please say you'll do it. Pleeease!"

"Well, the makeovers in *Gamma Girl* are my favorite part of the magazine," I mused. "But I'm not sure. What if I don't like what Julie does?"

"What's not to like? She looks perfect, and so do the Triple A's. Wouldn't you just love to look like them?"

"Actually, no."

"*Emily —*"

"*Gamma Girl* says to follow fashion, but be your own person at the same time. Wendy, I can't even tell any of them apart!"

"Pleeease . . ."

"Why don't you do it?"

"Because Julie picked you, not me. C'mon, Emily, haven't you ever wanted to be someone else? To just change everything and start over?"

There was a sharp knock on the door. Wendy opened it and Julie joined us. "Are you telling secrets?" she asked as she studied her invisible pores in the mirror.

"No," Wendy laughed nervously.

"That's good, because I'd hate to think you were talking about me. So, Emily, what's it going to be? Are you in or are you out?"

"I don't know . . ."

"Listen, anyone can see that you've got more fashion savvy than Ariana, Alyssa, and Ariel combined. All you need to work on is your looks, and that's easy enough because you're already pretty. You've got tons of potential, Emily. How about doing something for yourself? If you look good, you'll feel good."

Two minutes later, I found myself sitting on a bar stool as Julie slowly circled around me. I was excited and scared. The Triple A's stood nearby, each holding makeup or hairspray like nurses in an operating room. The other girls, including Wendy, watched from behind.

"We'll start by making a list of what's wrong with her," Julie said as she handed Betina a pad of paper. "Then we'll tackle the problems one at a time."

As the group shouted out my faults, I felt like I was shrinking. I knew from the makeover shows that you had to make the person look bad before they could look good. Still, it was painful. "Read the list back to us," Julie instructed.

Betina took a deep breath and began. "Thighs, stomach, arms, face, too heavy, left eyebrow thicker than right one, hair limp, skin pale, lips not plump enough, smile lopsided, cheeks undefined, too many freckles, and pimple on forehead."

"We've got a lot of work ahead of us," Julie said, frowning. "Okay, let's get started."

"Ouch!"

"Sit still, or it will hurt more," Julie ordered as she came at me with the tweezers again.

Even though I'm the main makeover project, Julie decided to try to help Wendy too. "Emily's not the only one who should lose some weight."

"I'm trying," Wendy wailed. When Julie looked at her sternly, she said, "But I can try harder."

Julie turned back to me. "Emily, you need to go on a diet *immediately*. You have great bone structure, but it's hidden under that baby fat. Once you shed some pounds, you're going to be amazed by how much better you look."

It was after 11 p.m. when Wendy's mom dropped me off. Alice was up working.

"Did you have fun?" Rats. I was trying to sneak into my room without being noticed. "Emily, come here."

I stuck my head into her office. Alice squinted and turned her desk lamp toward me. "Why is your hair so big? Your eyebrows look . . . different. Emily, are you wearing makeup?"

"Maybe."

"You know you're only allowed to wear lip gloss." I pursed my lips. "But I suppose since it was a party, you girls probably went crazy with Julie's mom's makeup. I remember when my friends and I used to play with our mothers' cosmetics."

I didn't tell Alice that it was Julie's makeup I was wearing.

"Libby gave me a piece of French silk pie to bring home. I could take a break and we could share it and talk," Alice suggested, pushing her chair away from the desk.

"Can't," I said, turning around.

"Why not?"

"I'm on a diet."

"A diet?"

"A diet."

"But Emily, you're not fat."

"If you can't fit into small sizes, then what's the point of even trying to look trendy?" I said, echoing Julie. "If I want to look good, I'm going to need to work at it."

"But you do look good, you look great, you always have."

"Alice, please," I said impatiently. "What do you know about style and fashion? I mean, come on. Look at how you're dressed."

Alice glanced down at her poncho and flared jeans. "It's comfortable," she said weakly.

I felt bad that I hurt her feelings. Still, she really has no fashion sense. I wish I could do a makeover on her.

Julie says that if I drop a few pounds and follow her beauty tips, I can be one of the prettiest girls at school. Me pretty? I've always considered myself fun, or crazy or carefree, but never pretty. Maybe I'll go along with Julie just a little bit. What can it hurt?

Emily

AUGUST 22

Dad,

Right before I left the house for Neighborhood Watch, Stanford called and hung up. I wish I had just hung up when that lady answered your phone. How is it that someone you don't even know can make you feel so miserable?

At first I thought that maybe, maybe, you'd call me after you unpacked from your tour. That is, if you are even back. I'm thinking that you must be because I'm not getting any postcards anymore, even though your poster has you listed for more concerts. As for the map, I still have a lot of stickers left. I'll save them, just in case.

But whatever. It's probably stupid of me to even hope you're going to call. Why would you? After you and Alice split for good, I hardly ever saw you. Sure, you'd do things with me when I asked. But once in a while it would have been nice if it had been your idea to get together.

As Alice and I patrolled the streets, I hoped that something exciting would happen. The biggest thing that's happened on our block since we moved here was when Mrs. Neederman's house was broken into and her oatmeal cookies were stolen. Later, it was discovered that her poodles had eaten them. There was indisputable evidence, Officer Ramsey told us. "Just ask the vet."

As we were shining flashlights into people's windows looking for signs of "suspicious behavior," Alice asked, "How are things with you and Millie?"

"I don't know."

"Have the two of you spoken lately?"

"No."

"Do you miss her?"

"I don't know."

"How do you feel?"

"I don't know."

Mrs. Neederman rushed out of her house when she saw us.

"Alice, Emily, look!" she cried. "I just got these photos. This is my daughter, you know, the one I told you about." Alice nodded and smiled as she aimed her flashlight on the photos. "And this is my granddaughter, Chloe." Mrs. Neederman turned to me. "You'd like Chloe. You remind me of her. She's a really nice girl. Chloe calls me all the time just to talk. She'll say, 'Gammy, I'm thinking of cutting my hair, what do you think?'"

"She's beautiful," Alice said, handing the photos back.

Just then Mrs. Neederman's poodles started barking. "Mommy's coming!" she called to them as she headed to the house.

We walked around the corner, and Alice slowed down. She seemed weary. "Look, Emily, I know you're mad at me and I don't blame you." I didn't say anything. "It seems like I've been mad at my mother for most of my life, and I wish things were different. Perhaps I haven't been as forthcoming as I should have been," she went on. "My mother never wanted me to marry your father. She thought that marriage to a musician was too unstable. Plus he wasn't Jewish. I didn't think it mattered, but apparently it did. We stopped talking once your father and I got married."

"What did Dad think of all this?"

"He thought that your grandmother and I were just being silly over something that wasn't a big deal."

"Was it a big deal?"

"It was to us. I don't think your father ever understood how sad it made me."

I wondered if Alice knows how sad I feel that the two of you aren't speaking.

"Why are you telling me this?" I asked.

"I don't really know. I guess when I saw how happy Mrs. Neederman's daughter and granddaughter made her, I wanted you to know why your grandmother hasn't been a huge part of your life. And that, well, sometimes I really miss my mom."

"Sometimes I miss my mom too," I whispered.

"What was that?"

"Nothing."

We walked some more in silence. Then I said, "Now that you're not married to that unstable non-Jewish musician anymore, maybe you could call her."

"It's not that easy. So much time has passed." She paused. "I'm not sure I can forgive her for not accepting your father. And I'm not sure she can forgive me for going against her wishes. But not a day goes by that I don't think about my mother."

Why do people stop talking when they aren't getting along?

Why doesn't Alice just call Grandma?

Why don't you just call me?
Why can't I call Millicent?
Why does Stanford call and hang up?
Why is everything so complicated?
Why?
Emily

AUGUST 23

Dear Dad,

This morning as Alice ate her granola and read the newspaper, she kept sneaking peeks at me.

"What?" I asked.

"Your eyebrows still . . . They . . . You . . ."

"I knooooooow," I moaned. I put down my glass harder than I meant to and milk splashed over the edge. "Just say it, just say that I look stupid!"

"I wasn't going to say that. I was going to offer to help you fix them."

Alice hardly ever wears makeup, but I've always been impressed with how well stocked her cosmetic drawers are. It was comforting to see her tattered bathrobe hanging behind the door, her toothbrush on the counter, and her clear orange face soap in the ceramic dish I made for her one Mother's Day.

Once, when I had to recite "Humpty Dumpty" in preschool, I stole Alice's soap. I kept it in my pocket, and when it was my turn to speak, I held on to it and it got me through the rhyme.

Alice kept rummaging through her drawers, pulling out things that didn't belong: a roll of red ribbon, a hammer, a pack of gum. "Here it is!" she finally said, holding an eyebrow pencil aloft.

As Alice filled in my eyebrows, our faces were only inches apart. She kept stepping back to examine her work, and then coming toward me again with the pencil. This time I didn't try to get away. It was the closest we had been all summer.

"There!" Alice stood back. "That's the Emily I recognize. You're beautiful. Really," she said, as if anticipating my protest, "eyebrows or no eyebrows!"

I wiggled my eyebrows at her and we both burst out laughing.

"Thanks, Alice," I said.

"You're welcome, honey. Say, why don't we go out for lunch today? There's a new Japanese restaurant called Uehara's I've been wanting to try."

"That would be nice," I said. "But I won't eat any eel or things with tentacles —"

Just then, the phone rang and startled both of us. It was Julie! "I'll take this in my room," I said.

"Hi, Emily."

"Hi, Julie!"

"Do you have lunch plans?"

"Ummm . . . no."

"Want to come to my house? A bunch of us are going to lunch later."

"Yes! Sure, that'll be fun!"

I rushed in to tell Alice. "Julie called and invited me to lunch!"

"Oh. I thought we were going to Uehara's?"

"Well, Julie's counting on me to show up. . . ." Alice looked sad and I hoped she wasn't going to start crying again. She's been so much better about not crying. "I hope you don't mind. I mean, I can cancel if you really want me to."

"No, no, you go right ahead," she said, putting on a smile. "We'll go to Uehara's another time."

"Great! Well, I've got to change. See you later!"

As I headed out I wondered if maybe I had been wrong about Julie. I've been wrong about a lot of people lately.

I was the first one to arrive.

"Emily, I'm so glad you're here," Julie said, ushering me into her room. There were clothes everywhere.

"Are you wearing a Felice Fashion belt?" I asked Julie.

"Yes!" she cried.

"And a Kirkpatrick Graffi-tee?"

"Yes!!"

"And a Castellucci Collection skirt?"

"YES!!!" she shouted. "Ohmygod, you know everything!"

I shrugged and tried not to look too pleased with myself. She was picking out her jewelry.

"This necklace, or this one?" she asked, holding them both up.

"The green one."

"Which earrings?"

"The dangly ones."

I was surprised when she followed my suggestions.

"Thanks for the advice. A friend never lets another friend leave the house looking bad." Then, even though no one was around, Julie lowered her voice. "Emily, can I tell you something?" She shut her door.

"Sure . . ."

"I want to be a fashion designer."

"You'd be great at that!"

"Really? You think so?"

I nodded.

"I've never told anyone that before," Julie confessed. "Please don't tell. I'm afraid people might laugh at me."

"But why? It makes perfect sense. You're like the most fashionable person I have ever met."

Now it was Julie's turn to blush. "Thank you," she said. "I am very fashion-oriented, it's true, and I can tell you are too. Alyssa, Ariel, and Ariana wouldn't recognize a Felice Fashion belt if Richard Felice himself handed them one."

Julie looked at me and suddenly began grinning. "Emily, I'm going to fix your hair! Don't say no, I want to do this."

Julie wouldn't let me see what she was doing, and was really serious the whole time. "You have nice hair, Emily. Have you ever considered highlights? Like a warm honey color? I could take you to Salon Ferrante. Mimi does the best color."

I had heard that highlights were expensive. But I did have a credit card. "Sure," I said. "Why not?"

Finally Julie said, "Voilà!" and walked me to her mirror. French braids. I've always wanted French braids!

When everyone arrived, we headed to Mel's for hot dogs.

"Love your hair," Wendy told me.

"Julie did it," I said proudly.

At Mel's, Wendy and I had diet sodas. The Triple A's shared a hot dog, and Julie got cheese fries, but she only ate a couple, then threw the rest away.

While we were there, a group of boys on skateboards came by and tried to flirt with us.

"How about a phone number?" the cute one wearing the helmet asked.

"How about no?" Julie said, flashing him her famous smile.

"You're killing me," he cried, clutching his heart.

Wendy and I grinned at each other. Then he turned to *us* and pleaded, "What about one of you lovely ladies? Care to help out a poor heartbroken skateboarder?"

We both started laughing, and he asked again. Finally I rattled off a phone number.

"Thanks, you just saved my life." He moved in closer to me and whispered, "And my reputation!"

As we watched him skate away with his friends, Julie said, "Emily, I can't believe you did that! Why would you do that? He wasn't even that hot."

"What makes you think I gave him my real phone number?" I asked.

Everyone cracked up, and Julie shrieked, "Emily Ebers, you are soooo bad!" Then we high-fived.

For the record, I didn't give him my real phone number, but I might have if I could have remembered it. I was so flustered that he even noticed me. It must have been the way Julie did my hair with her barrettes.

After Mel's, we went to the movies — the real movies where there are twelve theaters in one place, not the Rialto. While we were in the lobby, tons of girls and boys kept coming by to say hello to Julie and the Triple A's. It was like they were celebrities or something.

Wendy and I just stood to the side. Every now and then, Julie would remember to introduce me to someone. "This is Emily," Julie would say. "She's new."

Then I'd add, "And this is Wendy."

"I'm old," Wendy kept saying, until I told her to stop.

"So are you going to stick with the makeover?" Wendy asked as we walked past the concession stand.

"I think so," I said. I willed myself not to look at the Junior Mints or the Milk Duds or the Goobers.

"Oh Emily, this is so great!" Wendy whispered. She squeezed my arm as we entered the darkened theater. "We're going to be popular!"

Emily Ebers, popular person.

I could get used to that.

Emily

AUGUST 24

Dear Dad,

Today Alice and I went to the middle school for new student registration. I didn't want to be seen with her, but she claimed she had to sign a bunch of papers and prove we were residents by showing our cable bill and library cards. Does that mean if we don't watch television or read books, we're not really here?

When the registration lady looked over our paperwork and said, "Yes, you officially live in Rancho Rosetta, California!" I felt a twinge of pain. I used to tell people, "I live in Allendale, New Jersey." Now I can't say that anymore.

As Alice and I were registering for classes (well,

actually Alice was doing that, and I was just wishing she'd hurry up), I saw Julie coming our way. I stepped away from Alice.

"Emily!" Julie called out.

"Hi! What are you doing here?"

"You told me you had to register, so I thought I'd come by and show you around."

I tried not to grin too wide.

"Hello!" Alice said. "Emily, is this one of your friends?"

Instantly my grin disappeared.

"ThisismymotherAlice," I mumbled to Julie.

"Pleased to meet you," Julie said. "Would you mind if I showed Emily around school?"

"How nice. Yes, we'd love that," Alice answered. "Let me just finish up here. Emily, you get to choose an elective. How about photography? Remember those photos you took of Mercedes Metz's lawn gnomes?"

"Alice," I hissed, "Julie just wants to show *me* around school."

"Oh! Oh. Okay, well then. You two run along and have fun. I'll catch up with you later, Emily. I have to meet someone anyway. It was nice meeting you, Julie!"

As Julie and I took off, she turned to me and said, "What's with her crazy clothes?"

"It's research for an article she's writing," I said defensively.

For almost an hour, Julie and I roamed around school.

The campus is so big and there are trees everywhere. There are lots of cool, old buildings and a beautiful tile fountain in the middle of the courtyard. Julie says there's a rock-climbing wall in the gym.

"That bench is where the losers hang out.

"That's the make-out tree. It's where you go to show that you're in a serious relationship and don't care who knows.

"Those stairs are the ones where the popular kids gather. That's where we'll be."

It was so exciting being with Julie. I couldn't wait to tell Wendy. Oops! I just remembered that yesterday Wendy offered to show me around campus. Oh well, she'll understand.

As we crossed the street to the athletic field, Julie asked, "So Emily, how's the diet going?"

"I don't know if I can do it," I confessed. "It's a lot harder than I thought it would be."

"You're right, Emily. It is hard. Being popular is a lot more difficult than people think. I mean, look at me. Do you think looks like this appear by magic? No, I have to work on it. I play volleyball to keep in shape, I diet constantly, I TiVo all the hot shows, and I put up with Ariel, Alyssa, and Ariana. Plus half the school tries to imitate me, so I constantly have to reinvent my style to stay ahead of everyone. I'm also big on helping others, like always giving them fashion tips and pointers on how to look better."

I wondered if when Julie told me to stay away from bright patterns, she was trying to be helpful.

"Popularity is work. It really is," Julie said, sounding sincere.

"Is it worth it?"

"Well, yeah, of course it is. I can sit wherever I want in the cafeteria. Girls admire me. Boys go crazy around me. Even teachers like me. It's so totally worth it. I like to set goals. Like this year, I'm going to be the Winter Formal Queen, and I'm going to get Stanford Wong to be my boyfriend."

I felt my face burn red. Was it only a short time ago that *my* goal was to have Stanford Wong as my boyfriend? How deluded was I to think that something like that could ever happen? He never told me he was popular. It wasn't until Wendy explained who he really was that I figured it out.

Stanford still calls every day. It doesn't bother me like it used to. In fact, I actually get depressed when he doesn't call and hang up on me.

"What?" Julie asked. "Do you have a problem with Stanford?"

"Noooo," I said, hoping my voice didn't waver. "I barely know him."

"Well, he's the best basketball player the school's ever had. I've seen you talking to him. What's with that?"

"He knows Millicent."

"Who?"

"Millicent Min, from volleyball."

"Oh, her. Well, Stanford or Stretch, that's my big decision. I could easily go for Stretch too. In fact, I might. He is sooooo gorgeous and practically the only boy in school taller than me. But he doesn't talk, and Stanford and I talked all the time last year in Mr. Glick's English class.

"Stanford's the head of the Roadrunners and I'm the head of this group. They're the most popular boys, and we're the most popular girls, so it only makes sense for us to hang out together. Besides, he has five in his group and there are five of us. "

"Six."

"What?"

"There are six of us. You, me, Wendy, Ariel, Alyssa, and Ariana. That makes six."

Julie shook her head and gave me a pitying smile. "There are four of us who are already popular, one of us who will be popular when I'm through with her, and one who's more of a sidekick, if you know what I mean."

I was so glad Wendy wasn't there to hear that.

"Wendy's skinnier than you, and way better at volleyball. But she lacks that sparkle that you and I have. Plus we know fashion better than any of the other girls. It's so sad that they can't even tell the designers apart."

I was so glad I was wearing my John Gabby blue skirt, the one with the swirly pattern. I smiled back at her. It was like at that moment we totally connected.

"Well, I have to go now," Julie said as we walked out to the street and she slipped her sunglasses on. "My dad's taking my mom and me out to dinner tonight, so I have to get all dressed up. It's my mother's birthday. She's turning thirty-five again. My dad gave me some money to get her a gift, so I spent half of it on perfume and kept the other half since I don't think my allowance is big enough. Do you get an allowance?"

"My dad gave me a credit card," I mumbled.

"Wow!" Julie's eyes widened. "You are so lucky!"

She gave me a quick hug and headed down the street.

When Julie mentioned her mother's birthday dinner with her father, I thought about you. Not that I am expecting us to go out to dinner. In fact, I don't expect anything from you anymore. I'm not even sure why I'm still addressing this journal to you, except that it's gotten to be a habit. Remember that article Alice once wrote about bad habits being hard to break?

Well, even though your postcards have stopped and it's pretty clear you're not going to call, ever, at least I still have my credit card. When you sent it, I really thought things were going to change. I thought you had changed. I hoped you had. You remembered my birthday! Last year you didn't remember till you stopped by the house and saw the cake.

"Just a minute, I have something special for you," you said. Do you remember?

You ran to your car. When you returned you handed me a Bob Dylan CD and a ten-dollar bill. "Happy birthday, Emily, I think you'll like this." And I did like it because it was from you. I only wished the CD hadn't already been open. I still have the ten dollars, but I think I'll spend it tomorrow.

Emily

AUGUST 25

Dad,

This afternoon Wendy's mom drove us to the mall. Wendy's parents are nice, but they're just regular parents, not cool like Mr. and Mrs. Min.

"How's the diet going?" Wendy asked. She slammed the minivan door shut and waved good-bye to her mother.

"It's awful. I'm hungry all the time and all I can think of is food."

"I know," she moaned. "Me too."

"Why are you on a diet? You're already too skinny."

"Julie says I should lose five more pounds."

"Then you'll be invisible."

"You are so funny!" Wendy laughed. "You know, Julie really likes you. All I can think of is how great this next school year's going to be now that I'm hanging around with the popular girls!"

The air-conditioning hit us when we stepped into the mall. I hadn't realized how hot it was outside. Wendy spotted Julie first. She was in Sandberg's Shoe Emporium and had piles of sandals scattered around her.

"What about green, like a metallic green. Do you have these in green?"

"I'll see," the salesman said through gritted teeth.

"Emily!" Julie squealed when she saw me.

"Hi, Julie," said Wendy shyly.

"Come on." Julie jumped up and hooked her arm into mine. "We've got to meet Ariel, Alyssa, and Ariana. I want to show you something!"

Wendy looked unsure of herself until I said, "Come on, Wendy, join us."

"Wait!" the shoe salesman called out to Julie. "Miss! Miss, I have them in green — did you want to try them on?"

"You keep them," Julie laughed.

As we strolled through the mall, we passed a group of good-looking guys who looked like they were in high school. They checked Julie out. "Later, boys!" she said. Wendy and I glanced at each other. "I get that sort of thing all the time," Julie explained, shaking her head. "It gets old after a while."

The Triple A's were waiting for us in the purse section of Shah's.

"Well?" Julie asked.

"It was hard, but we did it," said Ariana.

"Mission accomplished," Alyssa or Ariel chirped up.

Julie glanced at the counter. "Good job." The Triple A's beamed.

Laid out neatly were three rows of purses.

"These are all the same," Ariana said, pointing to the row of six denim shoulder bags. "They're cool because you can put buttons and things on them."

"This row," explained Alyssa, "has different styles, but they are all basically the same size, and they are all brown, which is the new black."

"This one's the best," Ariel said, smiling. "Six identical purses, lots of side pockets, and all in different colors!"

"I like it." Julie nodded. The purses did look really nice. "I think we should get them. What do you think, Emily?"

"I love them," I said. "I just saw some purses like these in *Gamma Girl*."

"So we'd all get the same purse?" asked Wendy.

"That's the plan," said Julie.

"May I help you young ladies?" the Shah's saleswoman asked. She eyed all the purses on the counter.

"We're going to take these," Julie told her, motioning to the last row. Ariel beamed.

"All of them?" said the saleswoman.

"All of them," Julie answered.

"Well, they are somewhat expensive. . . ." The saleswoman hesitated. "Would you like to see Shah's line of more moderately priced bags?"

I stole a glance at the price tag. They were $112 each!

"That's okay," Julie said confidently. "Emily has a credit card."

What???

"Thanks, Emily," Ariel said. "That's really nice of you."

Ariana and Alyssa nodded.

Wendy looked worried. "Oh, that's okay, I already have a purse."

"Yes," Julie said. "But these all match. How cool is that? You do want to be cool like the rest of us, don't you? What do you say, Emily? Shouldn't Wendy be like us, or do you want her to be the only different one?"

Wendy looked flustered. "No, really, it's okay. These are really nice, but I can't afford it."

"That's okay," Julie assured her. "Emily's treating, aren't you, Emily?"

"I don't know," I stammered.

"We thought you liked us," Julie said. "I mean you've been hanging out at my house, and we've been doing the makeover on you and everything. I guess I thought you were our friend."

"I am your friend. . . ."

"Emily, I need to see you. Alone." Julie escorted me to the sunglasses display. As she tried on a pair, she said,

"I've been meaning to talk to you about Wendy. She's not really one of us, is she?"

"She's really nice," I said. I hoped she couldn't hear us.

"Yes, well, nice is not enough, is it? She's kind of bland, don't you think?"

"No . . ."

"That's so like you to stick up for her. It's one of the reasons I like you. You're very loyal, but you're rooting for the wrong team. It's us you ought to be loyal to."

"Julie . . ."

"Oh, all right, tell you what. If you get the purses, then maybe we'll let Wendy hang around with us. Who knows? Maybe she'll change. Maybe once we finish working on you, we'll take her on next."

"Excuse me?" the Shah's saleswoman called out. "Will you be purchasing these or not?"

"I don't know," Julie said, wandering back to the purses. "That's up to Emily. Emily, are we purchasing these purses?"

I looked from Julie to the saleswoman to Wendy.

"How much would that come to?" I asked. My voice was wobbly.

"Six hundred seventy-two dollars," the saleswoman replied. "Plus tax."

"Plus tax," I repeated. "Of course."

Six hundred seventy-two dollars. That's more than

I've ever spent on anything in my life. I thought about Julie's dad taking her and her mom out to dinner. Then I thought about the last time you, me, and Alice went out to dinner together, and how your postcards have stopped, and how you've called me only once this summer.

"Yes," I said. "Please charge them to my credit card."

"Oooh, thank you!" The Triple A's crowded around and hugged me. Wendy stood off to the side biting her nails.

Slowly, I opened my wallet. I felt weak. It was probably because I hadn't eaten anything all day.

Emily

AUGUST 26

Dear Dad,

I spent the morning in my room, watching a Shakespeare DVD I rented from Movie Mania. I thought Shakespeare was all about women in long dresses and men in tights, but in this movie they wore bathing suits most of the time. The description on the package said, "A fast and flashy modern-day retelling of an old classic. Set under the sizzling sun on Miami Beach, and with moonlit, mood-lit nights, you'll never forget this *Romeo and Juliet!*"

After the movie, I was hungry, so I went to Stout's for a bowl of soup.

"Is that all?" Libby asked. "How about a club sandwich and a slice of French silk pie?"

"I wish. No, just soup, please. And a glass of water."

After lunch, as I paid my bill, I handed Libby an extra five dollars. In exchange, she counted out twenty quarters. I went down the block and was about to put money in the parking meters, but I stopped myself. Instead, I turned around to tell Libby that she could have the quarters back if she needed them.

But when I approached Stout's, I spied Alice at the counter having a cup of coffee. Officer Ramsey was sitting next to her. They were laughing. Libby was laughing along with them, but Officer Ramsey kept looking at Alice. I thought you ought to know.

Even though I was early, Wendy was waiting for me on her front porch. She was wearing makeup and a new sundress. "Hurry," she said, rushing me toward Julie's house. "We can't be late."

"Nice dress," Julie said when she saw me. "Is it from Tavares Teens?"

"Nope, Jodi Jodi."

Julie nodded. "Even better."

As the Triple A's charted my progress, I recited what I had eaten the day before.

"You ate a cookie???!!!" Julie cried. "How could you?"

"I just bit into it," I said. "Then I chewed."

She shook her head, and so did Ariel and Alyssa. Or Ariana and Ariel, or Alyssa and Ariana.

"Emily, how are you going to lose that weight if you don't stick to your diet?"

"Well, maybe the diet isn't such a good idea," I said.

Wendy looked alarmed.

"The diet is a great idea," Julie informed me as she handed me a pair of tweezers. "Pluck."

"I'm not so sure. . . ."

"Sure it will hurt, but your eyebrows are still slightly uneven. It's not as hard as you think it will be. Just follow your natural arch."

"No, I mean the diet, and well, yes, the eyebrows and everything."

"Listen to me," Julie said. "If you look this good at the beginning of your diet, just imagine what you'll be like when you can fit into a size two! Think of all the new fashions you'll be able to wear."

The Triple A's murmured in agreement.

I'd be lying if I said I wasn't flattered. But a size two? Does that mean that the smaller I get, the more popular I will be? I've only been on this diet for a little while and I feel dizzy all the time. A two? I'm down to a nine/ten right now. I haven't been a two in ages. I'm getting head-aches. A two?

"When Emily loses her weight, she's going to look so hot in those new Parisi jeans," Julie said. "We won't even recognize her!"

I gave them a weak smile and didn't talk much the rest of the afternoon. If anyone noticed, they didn't say anything.

The more I think about it, the more mad I get at Julie for putting me up to buying those purses. But I am even madder at myself for letting it happen. Then I think about Wendy, and how much it means to her to be in Julie's group. And, well, I think about how starting at a new school as a popular girl is not a bad thing.

Wendy's nice. But it's just not the same as with Millie. Wendy doesn't read comics, and once when I hit her over the head with a pillow, she yelped, "Ouch! What did you do that for?"

Also, Wendy thinks the Rialto is hokey. "They only show old movies there," she said. "Most of them aren't even in color."

"Yes, but with the classics, once you get into them it doesn't matter what color they are," I explained.

Wendy does not have the appreciation for chocolate that Millicent and I share. And she doesn't have the same sense of humor, and sometimes our timing is just off, with these big gaps of awkward silence. I don't think Millie and I were ever silent. If anything, we both always tried to talk at the same time, we had so much to say to each other.

Still, I'm glad to have Wendy as a friend. She's not the kind of person who would ever take advantage of someone.

Emily

AUGUST 27

Dear Dad,

Wendy invited me to the movies with her family tonight, but Alice said I couldn't go. Lots of people are on vacation, so she volunteered us for extra Neighborhood Watches. Then, get this, tonight she was the one who was late.

"Where have you been?" I asked.

"Nowhere." She looked guilty. I didn't press. Lately Alice has been vague about where she goes. I'm not sure I want to know.

"Anything on your mind, Emily?" Alice asked as I dawdled by the front door. I really, really, really did not want to patrol the neighborhood. I wanted to be at the movies with Wendy.

"No."

"Because if there is, I'm here, you know."

Right. How could I not know? There's no avoiding her.

Mrs. Neederman walked by with her poodles and waved. We put on smiles and waved back. One of the poodles pooped on our lawn, but we all pretended not to see it.

As Mrs. Neederman disappeared into her house, the smiles slid off our faces and we began walking and not talking. Then Alice broke the silence.

"Emily, I'm concerned about this diet you're on. I

don't know if it's healthy. I think if you want to continue with this, you ought to see a doctor or a nutritionist —"

"Alice, I'm fine, okay?"

"No, not okay. Are you fine? Really? Because I'm not so sure. Emily, we need to talk. All right?"

"No."

"Listen, I'm telling you, this silent treatment you've been giving me all summer has got to stop!" Alice stood with her hands clenched at her sides. She raised her voice. "Emily, I just want to talk —"

"Talk? You want to talk? Okay, I'll talk!!!" My intensity startled both of us. "Why did you do it? Why did you leave him? Did you get tired of him? Were you jealous of Dad's band? Is that why? What's happening to us is all your fault! Don't you have any feelings at all? Don't you even care what you're doing to me?!!! You, you —"

"EMILY, STOP!"

I felt like I had been slapped in the face.

"Of course I care," Alice shouted. "I care more about you than you will ever know! Everything, everything I have ever done has been for you. I've turned down jobs to stay at home with you. I changed my life for you. Do you think that your father would do that?"

"Don't you say anything bad about my father! He loves me."

"I love you too, why can't you see that? Emily, you have got to hear me out!!!"

"Oh, I hear you all right. You're always talking about

the truth, how the truth is soooooo important. And then you lie to me. You say you love me, and you used to say that to Dad too. Yet you tore us all apart. Why? Why did you ask him for a divorce? I know it was you. He told me! Why can't you just tell the truth for once?"

"Hey," a man's voice shouted. "Stop yelling! I'll call Neighborhood Watch if you don't quiet down!"

Alice plopped down on the curb and turned off her flashlight. Her head dropped and her shoulders slumped forward like she had suddenly crumbled.

I was scared.

"The truth. The truth," she finally said, sounding flat. "Okay, I can do that. Ask me anything."

I took a deep breath. "I need to know how long you and Dad knew you were getting a divorce before you told me. I need to know why you did it. I need to know why all this happened and if I will ever feel better again."

I could feel my heart beating fast.

"Oh, honey," Alice murmured as I sat down next to her. "You will feel better eventually. When exactly, I'm not sure. But you will. You are so strong, and I admire that. I always have."

It was a while before she spoke again, and for once I was afraid she wasn't going to have anything else to say.

"No one ever wants their marriage to end," she began slowly. "But sometimes it happens. With your father and me, well, there were circumstances that we could not get over. Your father didn't want to grow up, and according to him, I became too tense and rigid. He said I wasn't fun anymore. I think he just lost interest in me. I kept thinking things would change, but they didn't. We knew it was over about six months before we told you. I wanted to tell you sooner, but your father kept putting it off."

"How could you keep this from me for so long? Why did you?"

"I can't speak for your father, but I guess I kept hoping things would change. Or that they weren't as bad as I thought they were. I was in denial."

"Was it really your idea to get divorced?"

"I did ask for a divorce, but I never thought he'd agree to it. I asked him because I wanted to hear him say, 'Alice, why would we ever do something like that? We can work this out, I know we can.' Only my plan backfired, and instead, he said, 'Yes, I think that would be best.'"

"Emily, I am so sorry. We never meant to hurt you. You need to know that the divorce has nothing to do with you."

"Wrong," I said, my voice shaking. "You are so wrong. You think your divorce has nothing to do with me? It has everything to do with me. What did you expect? That I wouldn't take it personally? This divorce has turned my life upside down. And when I try to love either of you, I feel like I'm hurting the other person and I can't stand that!"

"Emily," Alice stammered, "please don't feel that way. You are the best thing that came out of our marriage. Your father and I both want you to be happy. We would never deliberately hurt you."

Neither one of us moved, but I felt as though I was about to explode.

"Then why did you make me pick?" I whispered.

"What was that?"

"You made me pick." I realized I was crying. How long had I been crying? "You and Dad made me pick who I wanted to live with! How unfair is that? Do you remember how much I cried when you said I had to choose?"

"I remember."

"Why did you do that to me?"

"We just thought that you should have some say. . . ."

I couldn't listen to her anymore. I was on total overload. I ran home, but the door was locked. I pounded on it even though I knew no one would answer. By the time Alice arrived with the keys, my fists hurt and I was exhausted. She opened the door without saying anything and I went straight to my room.

"Emily?" I heard her call out. "I am sorry. For everything. I love you."

Alice was on the other side of the door. I wanted to open it, but something was stopping me from letting her in.

"Me too," I said. But I don't think she heard me.

When I think about Alice I feel frustrated and fed up.

When I think about you I feel unsettled and unsure, and that's worse. For the record, I picked Alice because I knew you wanted to get the Talky Boys back together and go on the road. If you had to stay with me, you couldn't have done that. I would have gotten in your way. But when I did pick, you didn't even pretend and say, "No, I want Emily to live with me." Instead you said, "Well, I guess she's made her choice."

I felt like Alice needed me more. But the sad thing is, I need both of you. I need you to be back together. I need my life to be exactly the same as it was one year ago, when everything was good, and when Nicole and A.J. and I had our best summer together, and when you were happy because you sold that expensive house, and Alice was happy because she won that journalism award. And I was happy, because I had no idea what was coming.

Emily

AUGUST 28

Dad,

Alice and I spent the morning avoiding each other, which wasn't hard, since we had so much practice over the summer.

I was startled when the phone rang.

"Hello?" I said.

Silence.

"Hello? Is anyone there?"

"Hi, it's me!"

"Me who?" I said, even though I could see who it was from caller ID.

"Millie, silly."

I wasn't sure what to say. We hadn't spoken in so long.

"What do you want, Millicent?"

"Well, I just thought that unless we both could afford the airfare to the Hague to the International Court of Justice . . ."

Before, when Millicent said weird things, I just thought she was odd. Now it was obnoxious.

"Millicent," I interrupted, "*what* are you blabbing about?"

When she didn't answer for the longest time, I was afraid she had hung up.

"I want to be friends again," she said softly. "I'm sorry for whatever misunderstanding there was."

Millie was saying the words I longed to hear. Only she couldn't just stop at that. "I'm sorry you cannot comprehend my being a genius and a senior in high school —"

"You still don't get it, do you?"

Alice wandered into the kitchen. She looked tired and her dashiki was inside out. "Who is it?" she asked.

"Nobody," I said, covering the phone.

"Is it the cable TV man?"

"I said, it's *nobody*."

"If it's the cable TV man, tell him that HBO doesn't work anymore but that we still get Showtime."

"I can't talk," I hissed to Millicent.

"Emily, please," she begged, "can we at least meet? I promise not to take more than ten minutes of your time."

I gave this some serious thought. Did I really want to meet with Millicent Min? After all this time, it felt awkward talking to her. It had never felt that way before. "Okay," I finally agreed. "Meet you in half an hour. The mall. Our regular place."

As usual, Millicent was waiting for me in the food court. She was wearing her favorite "So many books, so little time" T-shirt, her briefcase at her feet. I took a hard look at it. It wasn't a faux briefcase. It was the real thing, and it didn't look trendy, it looked geeky.

"Hi Emily!" Millie's voice was wobbly but her body was stiff. She handed me a big bag of Jelly Bellies. I love Jelly Bellies, especially the bubble gum and licorice flavors.

"No thank you." I pushed the bag away. "I'm on a diet."

Millie's jaw dropped. "But you're not fat! Anyway, jelly beans are fat-free."

"I am on a diet," I repeated firmly as I pulled out a chair. It made an embarrassing sound as it scraped against the floor. Normally one of us would have cracked a joke about this. Instead, I sat down and crossed my arms. Millicent remained standing. She was wearing two friendship necklaces, hers and mine, and she clutched both as she spoke.

"Well, I know that my being a genius can be off-putting," she began. "But I am certain our friendship is strong enough to withstand the effects of my high intelligence."

"Man," I said, shaking my head, "for someone who's supposed to be so smart, you sure are dumb."

"Pardon me?"

"Millicent," I struggled to explain, "this is not about your brain. I'm mad at you because we were supposed to be best friends! But you didn't trust me enough to tell me the truth. Instead, you just assumed I wouldn't be able to handle it. There was this huge part of your life that you hid from me!"

"I can't believe you just called me *dumb*! *Et tu, Brute*."

"But Millie, you do act really dumb sometimes, like you're clueless." By now we were both standing.

"So . . . ?" Millie was gripping the beads so hard, I was afraid the necklaces would break.

"So nothing. It doesn't matter to me."

"Really?"

"I don't care if you're smart or dumb, as long as you're a true friend."

Millicent was silent for the longest time. Finally she

said, "Emily, I'm sorry if I misrepresented myself in any manner. For you see, I had sorely misjudged the dynamics of our relationship. . . ."

Urggggg, why was she making this so hard?

"Millie, you just didn't misjudge our relationship, you misjudged me!" I shouted. "Can't you just shut up and say you're sorry you lied without making up a bunch of hooey?"

Instantly I was sorry. Millie looked the way I felt — hurt.

Finally after a million years, she mumbled, "I am sorry I lied to you, Emily. I hope you can forgive me."

Could I forgive her? I wondered. After her lies and betrayal? Now it was up to me. I could go on being angry at Millicent and feeling horrible. Or I could be her friend again. My body suddenly got light and I was dizzy, but this time it wasn't from not eating.

Millie let go of the necklaces as she turned to walk away.

"Hey!" I grabbed her shirt. "Where do you think you're going? I really missed you." I gave her a bear hug and she hugged me back. "I always knew you were strange," I said as I took the bag of Jelly Bellies and dipped into them. (They tasted sooooooo good!) "But I could never figure out why. Now I think I know. It's because you're an only child, isn't it? Alice thinks that because I don't have brothers or sisters it has affected my outlook on life. She also finally admitted that she should have told me about the divorce sooner. And get this, she is STILL wearing those weird hippie clothes —"

"Emily," Millie interrupted. "I need to ask you something."

"Yes?"

"What happened to your eyebrows?"

"Oh. Well, you're not going to believe this, but I plucked them. I know, they look hideous. . . ."

As I started to explain, Millie did something very un-Millicent. She burst into tears.

"They'll grow back," I assured her.

"It's not that. I'm just so happy we're friends again. Oh, Emily, I missed you so much. Things just didn't feel right when you weren't around."

"I felt the same way! But Millicent, we're not back to normal. You know that, don't you?"

"What do you mean?" She looked worried.

I pointed to my friendship necklace. "I want mine back, or I'll have to wrestle you for it," I said.

She broke into a huge grin, took the beads off her neck, and placed them around mine.

Soon we were both sobbing so loud that the man eating a burrito at a table nearby got up and left. I remember crying like this in Mrs. Buono's class when I was leaving all my friends behind. Only this time, I wasn't saying good-bye. I was saying hello.

Emily

AUGUST 29

Dear Dad,

I picked up some Moon Pies at the store this morning. When I got home, Alice was talking to someone in her office.

"I was thinking of teaching at Rogers College."

"That's where I'm going to summer school. Maybe I could introduce you to Professor Skylanski. . . ."

"Look who's here!" Alice called out when she saw me.

"MILLIE!" I shouted.

We grabbed a couple of sodas and retreated to my room. It was just like old times, except that about every ten seconds we would grin at each other for no reason. I told her all about Julie and Wendy and the Triple A's.

"Did you want her to do the makeover on you?" Millie asked.

"Yes and no. I sort of didn't think I had a choice," I said. "What did you do when we weren't together?"

"I read a lot," Millie said, biting into a Moon Pie. "And I helped Ms. Martinez organize the library storage room. It was scary back there."

"Did you ever read *Romeo and Juliet*?"

"Of course."

"Well, what did you think of it?"

"I liked it, especially Act Two, Scene Two, even though it is grossly overquoted. You know" — she stood on a chair and put her hands over her heart —

O Romeo, Romeo! Wherefore art thou Romeo?
Deny thy father and refuse thy name;
Or, if thou wilt not, be but sworn my love
And I'll no longer be a Capulet.

"Oh! I love that scene too. And what about when Juliet fakes her death? Wasn't that unreal? Didn't you just want to scream, 'Not a good idea!'"

"Yes! And when she wakes up to find Romeo dead. Oh, the irony!"

"I cried until Juliet splashed water on him and yelled, 'Awaken!' And then they did that shimmy dance on the beach!"

"'Awaken'?"

"Yeah, and that dance with floaties and beach umbrellas."

"Are we talking about the same thing?"

"*Romeo and Juliet.*"

"Right, the Shakespeare play. Emily . . . did you *read* the play?"

"Well, I watched it," I confessed. "Alice really wanted me to read it this summer. . . ."

". . . for her Shakespeare in inner-city schools article."

"I couldn't get through it, so I rented the movie. *Romeo and Juliet: Wavelength.*"

"That explains a lot of things," Millie snorted.

"Have you ever read *The Outsiders*?"

"Of course. It's got shades of *Romeo and Juliet*, and plenty of teenage angst."

"Stanford gave it to me. I never finished it. Does it have a happy ending?"

"I'm not going to tell you. You're going to have to read it for yourself."

"I thought you'd say that. You know," I said softly. "This might sound funny, but at one time I really thought Stanford Wong liked me."

"He did like you." Millie said, picking up a Bob Dylan CD. "He still does." *What?* "I was hoping Stanford would call you. Has he?"

"Well, he's called me about a thousand times, but he never says anything."

"That coward! Stanford was embarrassed to have you find out he needed a tutor. It was his idea to pretend he was tutoring me."

I shook my head. "What is wrong with the two of you?"

As Millicent continued alphabetizing my CDs, Alice knocked on the door.

"Emily, there's a call for you." She paused. "It's your father."

My father!!!!

I was so happy to hear from you! I couldn't stop grinning.

"Daddy!!! Daddy, I've missed you so much!"

"Me too, pumpkin. Listen, Emily, there's something I have to tell you."

At last! I thought. I smiled knowingly, as I waited for you to clear up if you were still on tour, why the postcards stopped, who that lady was. . . .

"Emily, I need you to stop using the credit card," you said. "I just got a call from the credit card company asking me to confirm the purchase of six purses. Did you buy six purses?"

"Yes, but —"

"Emily, there's no excuse for something like that."

"But —"

"And it's not just the purses. It looks like as the summer's gone on, you've started spending more and more. You're thirteen years old, you ought to know better."

"I'm twelve."

"Oh. Well, twelve is old enough to know better."

"Are you still on the road?" I asked.

"Er, well. Yes, no. We're sort of on a hiatus. We were on the road, but the tour was cut short. The promoters didn't do their jobs, and, well, it wasn't our fault the crowds weren't there."

"Why didn't you call me when you got back?"

"I've been meaning to, but well, you know. Things get busy. We're putting together a new show. This one will be so much better. New material too. Not just those oldies. Luka's working on a power ballad that we think has number one written all over it, and Dean just got a new Gibson. . . ."

"You only called once the entire summer."

"Oh. Uh, I kept meaning to. But the band and all . . ."

"Right. The band."

Now that you were finally on the phone, I couldn't wait to hang up. *Emily, I need you to stop using the credit card,* you said.

Emily, I need you to stop using the credit card.

Emily, I need you to stop using the credit card.

"Uh, Dad, I gotta go."

"Sure, okay. I love you, Emily."

"Yeah. Love you too."

The tears started before there was a dial tone. I couldn't breathe. Alice rushed into the room. She was crying too.

"It's not your fault, it's not your fault," she murmured.

It felt so good to be hugged. But when Alice kept crying, it was more than I could take. Her tears were drowning me.

"Please," I begged, "you have to leave."

Alice sucked in a sharp breath. "Oh. Yes, all right. I'll go. But Emily, if you need me, I'm always here."

I nodded as I shut the door after her.

Millie looked uncomfortable.

"I thought he called to tell me he was coming back," I tried to explain through my tears. "Or that he wanted to say he had made a mistake. But nooooooo, Daddy just called because he wants me to stop using the credit card."

"You do know that you were being delusional by thinking you could just will him to call and say everything you wanted to hear?"

I looked up at her. "Of course I knew it wasn't going to happen, but I can pretend, can't I? And what is your problem? You're supposed to be my best friend, not a balloon popper."

"A balloon popper?"

"Bubble burster, party pooper, balloon popper, whatever. Stop being so logical!"

Millicent grew quiet as she handed me tissue after tissue, until I ran out of tears. "Say, Em." She hesitated. "Why don't you do that makeover on me you've always wanted to do?"

"Really?"

Millicent nodded.

"Okay," I said. The tears started up again. "That will be fun."

Millie never let me do a makeover on her before, no matter how much I begged. And now she was asking for one? I knew why. It was because she's my best friend in the entire world. After almost an hour, I told Millie to face the mirror. It wasn't quite like *Marieke's Makeover Madness*, but Millicent did look pretty good, and even said so herself.

As Millie was admiring herself in the mirror, Alice came back. She had pulled herself together.

"Just checking to see how you're doing," she said.

"I'm fine, Alice, *okay?*"

She looked at Millicent, who was still staring at the mirror and making scowling faces like a model. "Interesting," Alice murmured.

"Alice, *please.*" I hoped she wouldn't embarrass Millie.

"It's not how you look that's important, it's how you feel," Millie announced. "And I feel great."

"It's not how you look . . ." Alice repeated as she left.

As I packed my bag for a sleepover at Millie's, I looked around the room at all the things you got for me this summer. Well, you didn't really get them for me, I just pretended that you did. I'm sorry about the purses. I'll pay you back somehow. You once told me that the credit card was for little things and emergencies. I guess at the time, getting those purses was an emergency.

Now, I realize I couldn't be the person Julie wanted me to be, any more than you could be the person I wished you were. Because as hard as it is to change yourself, it's even harder to change someone else.

When I walked into the living room, I was surprised to find Millie talking to a stranger. As I got closer, I realized who it was. It was my mother, not Alice the hippie, or whoever she's been this summer, and she was wearing her favorite gray tracksuit and beat-up sneakers.

"I was a terrible hippie," Alice said to me.

"Yes, but you're not a bad mom," I told her.

"Are you okay, Emily?"

Was I okay?

"I'm fine." I kissed her cheek. "Are you okay?"

"I will be," she said.

"Me too," I answered. And for the first time all summer, I really felt like I would be.

Emily

AUGUST 30

Dear Diary,

Starting today, this journal is no longer addressed to my father. That's because I've decided not to send it to him. He wouldn't be interested. So instead, from this day forward, it will be addressed to Dear Diary.

Dear Diary,

Today, Millie and I stopped to visit Maddie. Her house was practically empty since she's leaving for England in two days. Julius was resting in the middle of the living room. He was wearing a Lakers cap.

"The cap was a gift from a good friend," Maddie explained. "Now, ladies, how about some cookies and lemonade? Cookies and lemonade should always be the last thing you pack, just in case some VIPs drop by."

"I'll get it," Millie offered.

As she disappeared into the kitchen, I set down my backpack and turned to Maddie. "Remember when you read my tea leaves? What did it mean, when you said it was up to me to decide where my journey would take me?"

"Sometimes we have no choice in what happens to us," Maddie said, putting the Lakers cap on my head. "Other times we can guide our futures, or at least help them along. Like with feng shui, this ancient Chinese practice gives people the opportunity to flourish. Stagnant water grows moss, free-flowing rivers move forward. You can't be lost if you know where you are."

"Maddie," I said solemnly, "I have no clue what you are talking about."

"Half the time I don't either, but it sure sounds good, doesn't it?"

She took my hand in hers. "Oh! You've drawn another cute face," she said. I blushed. Maddie opened my palm and traced the lines on my hand with her finger. "Emily, you're almost home. Keep moving forward and you'll eventually find your way."

"How will I know when I'm there?"

"You'll know."

"And then my journey will be over?"

Maddie laughed and gave me a hug. "If you're lucky

your journey will never be over. But whether you enjoy it is up to you."

"How did you get so wise, Maddie?"

She leaned in and whispered softly, "Vitamins."

After finishing off the last cookie, I gave Julius his Lakers cap back.

"Are you going to miss Maddie?" I asked Millie as we headed to her house.

"I already do," she said.

When we were in her room I pulled my Elmo tape recorder out of my backpack. "This should cheer you up," I said. "It's my dad."

"Your dad is a plastic Elmo?"

"No! My dad is on the tape recorder. Listen, this is him singing when I was little." I played "The Emily Song." "He wrote that especially for me."

"He has a good voice. What's on the rest of the tape?"

"Nothing, just me trying to talk when I was little. I only listen to my dad's song. It's all I have left of him."

Millicent groaned. "You're quite the drama queen, Emily!"

That made me smile. "Yeah, I guess I am."

"I want to hear baby Emmie!" Millie said as she grabbed Elmo and pressed play. We howled at my baby babble. I was amazed that I ever sounded like that.

"You have no problem talking now," Millicent assured me.

I threw a pillow at her, then continued reading my Archie as we listened to my gibberish. Finally the babbling stopped. I picked up the tape recorder to rewind it, but before I could hit the OFF button, a new voice came on.

"Hi, little sweetheart. You're taking a nap right now. I hope you're having sweet dreams." It was Alice. "I love you so much. I want you know that I will always be here for you, no matter what. That's a promise."

Why had I never heard that before?

"She's so nice," Millie noted. "So are you, except for . . . never mind."

"What?"

"Nothing."

"Pleeeeease tell me!"

"Well, I know I've said this before, but I'm not sure why you never talk to your mom. I think she's really lonely."

"She told you that?"

"No, but I can tell. She turned down a really great assignment in Paris so she could be with you this summer."

"She did? How do you know?"

Millie was silent.

"How do you know?" I pressed.

"Sometimes when she's not around, I look at things in her office," Millicent mumbled.

"You *snoop*?"

"That's not important. The important thing is that Alice misses you." Millie looked guilty. "You're not going to tell her I went through her things, are you?"

"No, I'm not going to say anything."

"Phew! For a moment I thought you were mad at me."

"It's not you I'm mad at."

"Don't tell me you're mad at Alice again. It's a little superfluous."

"Well, she can be so pushy. Like insisting that we talk all the time. And she was always forcing my dad to take me places, then she'd pretend it was his idea."

"So, you're mad at her because she cares about you and wanted your father to be a bigger part of your life? Oh yeah. I can see why you hate her."

"I never said I hated her. I don't hate her. . . ."

"Listen, Emily, we never know how long we have with a person. Your grandpa could die, your grandmother could leave, your mom could be hiding a major medical condition —"

"What? Are you trying to tell me something?" Millicent wouldn't look at me. "Ohmygosh! You found something when you were snooping, didn't you? Something's wrong with Alice!"

Millie scrunched up her face. "Nothing's the matter with her," she said unconvincingly.

All of a sudden I had to talk to Alice. It was as if my

emotions were suffocating me and the only person who could save me was my mother. I couldn't breathe.

"Hey, where are you going?" Millicent called after me.

"There's someone I need to talk to," I yelled back.

Even though volleyball hadn't turned me into Olympic material, it had gotten me into better shape. I ran home. When I turned the corner, my heart stopped. A police car was parked in our driveway. I raced inside to find Alice sprawled out on the couch, her eyes closed.

Just then, Officer Ramsey walked in from the kitchen with a glass of water. I grabbed it and threw the water at Alice.

"AWAKEN!!!" I ordered.

Alice bolted upright and screamed.

"Um, Alice, do you still want the aspirin?" Officer Ramsey asked.

"Emily?" she sputtered.

I burst out crying. "I thought . . . I thought you . . ."

"Oh, honey," Alice said, "it's just a small headache, certainly not enough to kill me. I think it's my sinuses again. Officer Ramsey was kind enough to give me a ride home from the library."

When I didn't stop crying, she reached out to me and I met her halfway. At first it was awkward, but soon I relaxed, and it felt good to lean on her. Every time I hugged Alice just a little tighter, she returned the hug. It was like we were in our own world, and it wasn't until

Officer Ramsey spoke that I remembered someone else was in the house with us.

"Alice, is this you in the bat mitzvah photo?" Officer Ramsey was pretending to be interested in the photo on our fireplace mantel. "I can't remember anything about my bar mitzvah, except at one point I fainted."

By then Alice and I were both weeping. Officer Ramsey coughed and said, "Well, I guess I'll just show myself out. Er, hope you feel better soon, Alice. Good-bye, Emily."

"I'm so sorry," I sobbed when the door shut. I grabbed a cushion to blot my tears.

"It's okay, my clothes will dry. It was just water."

"No, I mean about this summer and life and everything. I've been so mean to you," I blubbered.

"That's true," she said.

"Well, you were pretty much a basket case, you know."

"That's true too!"

Alice put her hands on my shoulders and looked into my eyes. "Listen, Emily, I have some things to tell you. And I'm not giving you a choice this time. You're going to listen to me, okay?"

I nodded.

Alice took a deep breath. "No more lies. You're old enough to know the truth. Your father and I did you a real disservice by thinking you couldn't handle knowing the divorce was coming, when really it was us who couldn't handle it. Believe it or not, parents don't always know the right thing to do."

"Ooooh, I believe it!"

Alice smiled for a moment. "Things are going to change around here, for the better." She took a deep breath. "I've started seeing someone. . . ."

"I know. Officer Ramsey."

She blushed. "No, I've started seeing a psychologist and she's been really helpful. I think it's time for me to move forward with the rest of my life."

"Can I go with you?"

Alice squeezed my hand. "I would love that. But first, I think I'd better change out of these wet clothes!"

It wasn't our night for Neighborhood Watch, but we went for a walk anyway — just a regular walk, no flashlights, though out of habit, we kept peering into our neighbors' houses.

"Emily, are you angry that I made you move?"

"I was. Sometimes I still am. But I'm getting used to the idea. I'm a little worried about school starting."

Alice nodded. "New situations can be scary. They can also be invigorating. Emily, I have always admired the way you tackle life."

"The way I tackle life? What, like I'm a football player?"

"No," she laughed. "You've always had such a great sense of who you are. Like when you got the title role of *Annie*, and Nicole was your understudy. But you insisted you'd rather play an orphan, so Nicole got the lead."

"Well, I knew how much she wanted that part."

"That's what I mean. You stepped aside so that someone else could be in the spotlight. You didn't need the lead role in a play to feel important."

We walked in silence for a while. "Why didn't you go to Paris?" I asked.

"You knew about that?"

I nodded. "You could have gone, you know. I heard it was a really big assignment."

"It was. A cover story. But I'd much rather be with you. What's Paris, when I could spend a summer with my daughter?"

Just then Officer Ramsey pulled up alongside us. "Hello again!"

"Hello!" we both said as we kept walking.

"Beautiful evening, isn't it?" He drove the car slowly to keep pace with us.

"It really is," Alice agreed. "More than I could ever wish for."

"How's your headache?"

"It's gone now."

Officer Ramsey just gazed at her for a long time, and then said, "Okay, well, I'd better go make sure Rancho Rosetta is safe. Take care, both of you!"

"He's not bad," I said as his car turned the corner.

"Not bad at all," Alice said.

We didn't say much after that. We didn't need to. The fact that we were walking arm in arm said it all.

AUGUST 31

Dear Diary,

This afternoon I called Julie. She sounded sleepy even though it was after 2 p.m. "Sure, come on over," she yawned. "I'm glad you called, I want to show you some things."

A few days ago I would have been thrilled to hear her say she was glad to hear from me. Today it meant nothing. I may have been slow, but I finally figured out what a true friend is, and Julie never was one.

Julie's mom answered the door. She was wearing high heels. Julie says she always wears high heels, even to the grocery store. "You're looking good," she said. "It must be that diet!"

"I'm not dieting anymore," I told her. "Ever."

Julie was in her room, sprawled in a beanbag chair. The Triple A's floated in and out of the room, carrying diet sodas and laughing at their own jokes. Wendy was on the floor studying a photo album. Everyone ignored her.

"Hi Emily!" Wendy said, grinning.

Julie held up a catalog. "Look! These necklaces are so cute! I think we ought to consider getting them. What do you think, Emily? They're so much cuter than those plastic beads you're wearing."

"You're wrong, these beads are beautiful. And as for the necklaces in the catalog, I think they're great.

Only you're going to have to get someone else to pay for them."

Julie's smile never wavered. "Is there something you're trying to tell me?"

Wendy's eyes darted from me, to Julie, then back to me.

"I'm just saying that it's not nice to take advantage of someone."

"Who's doing that?" asked Julie.

"You know who."

"Emily . . ." Wendy began.

"Stay out of this," Julie ordered. "Look, Emily, if you're talking about the purses, big deal. It wasn't even your money, it was your dad's. He won't care."

"How do you know?"

"I know how dads are."

"Then why don't you get your dad to buy your things?"

For a split second, Julie's smile turned into a frown. "Listen, Emily. You seem to have forgotten everything that I am doing for you. Not just anyone can get into my group. That I took you on is a miracle. Betina even asked why I was letting you hang around since you're so fat."

I flinched. "I am not fat," I growled. "I am within the healthy guidelines for my weight! Just ask any doctor."

Wendy stood up. "She's not fat!" When Julie shot her a glare, Wendy sat back down and added meekly, "Well, she's not."

Julie cupped her ear. "What? Is the mouse saying something?" She faced me. "Because I am a generous person, I will give you a chance to apologize."

Silence.

"I'm waiting . . ."

"I'm sorry," I finally said.

"I thought so!" Julie winked at me. "Now, about those necklaces . . ."

"No!" I cut her off. "I'm sorry you're the way you are. I think it's you who owes Wendy and me an apology. And while you're at it, you ought to apologize to Millicent Min too, for all the mean things you've said to her this summer."

Julie rose from the beanbag and stretched to her full height. "Excuse me?"

"You know, Julie," I said. "It's not that hard to be nice. I've even seen you do it, like when you showed me around school. You should do it more often. You might even like it."

The Triple A's were as stiff as mannequins. Julie shook her head. "I tried to help you, Emily. And this is how you thank me?"

"Thanks, Julie," I said. "I appreciate the makeover, but I've decided to go back to being plain old me."

As I headed to the door, Wendy called out, "Emily, wait for me!" She was quiet as we walked away from Julie's house.

"Well, that was sort of fun in a weird way," I said.

"We're dead," Wendy lamented. "Julie's going to kill us when school starts. We might as well drop out right now."

"We'll protect each other," I told her. "Julie's not scary, unless you let her get to you."

"It was fun being in the popular group while it lasted," Wendy sighed. "But you know, hanging around with Julie was nothing like I thought it would be. She was actually sort of dull. And they call my friends boring!"

"You're not boring," I said to Wendy as we parted.

"You know what?" she replied. "I'd pick you for a friend over Julie any day."

When I got home I was happy to find Millie with Alice at the dining room table. They were eating sandwiches and there was a place set for me. I was starving.

"We were just talking about the Fiesta," Alice said.

I bit into my sandwich. It was delicious — roast beef, avocado, cheese, onions.

"The whole town turns out for the end-of-summer Fiesta at Wild Acres Theme Park," Millicent explained. "Which is why we shouldn't go. It will be too crowded."

"Are you kidding me? We've got to go!" I told her. I took another bite. "Where'd you get the sandwiches?" I asked Alice.

"I made them," she said.

I smiled. "They taste great. Hey, why don't you come to Wild Acres with us?"

"I would love to, but I'm on a deadline. But Emily," she said, "please ride a roller coaster for me, okay?"

"Okay!"

As I neared Wild Acres with the Mins, I could hear the music and the screams and the laughter blending together.

"C'mon, what are we waiting for?" I shouted. I raced to get in line at Monstroso, the giant roller coaster. "Millie, hurry!"

As we boarded the coaster, my stomach was all butterfly-ish. Millie looked terrified and kept testing her seat belt. Mr. Min kept practicing raising his hands high in the air. It looked like he was doing arm exercises.

"Good luck," the roller coaster man growled. "Hope I see you when it's over. The last time around we lost four riders."

"Really?" I squealed.

"That didn't happen," Millicent started to say, but she choked on her sentence as Monstroso started chugging up the track. I loved the view from the top. For the first time I could see all of Rancho Rosetta. Everything looked different, better, more beautiful from a distance —

"Aaaaaaaaaaaaaaaaaaaaaaaaaaaaaaaaahhhhhhhhhhhhhhhhhh!!!!!"

Millie and I screamed our heads off. When Monstroso finally slowed to a stop, Mr. Min and Millicent hugged and we all agreed it was the best ride ever. Then Millie and I took off on our own.

It had occurred to me that Stanford Wong might be at Wild Acres. I was wearing my good-luck jeans and my new Jodi Jodi purple top. I even used my White Lightning perfume, but just a dab like they say in *Gamma Girl*. And I held on to my friendship necklace.

"Let me know if you see him, okay?"

"Emily, he's a doofus of the highest order. I can't believe you still like Stanford, knowing that he's just a stupid boy," Millicent said as we pushed our way through the crowd.

"I still liked you when I thought you were a stupid girl. Besides, I don't think he's stupid. You can't be stupid and play basketball as well as he does," I told her. "What I don't understand is why he never apologized. I thought he liked me."

Millie gave me a stern look. She'll make a really good mom someday. "Excuse me, but haven't we been over this a billion times? He does like you, he likes you a lot. Okay???!! Now can we *please* change the subject? Sheesh."

As we neared the stage, I could hear music. A group of old guys was playing. They were good, but not nearly as good as the Talky Boys. As I scanned the audience for Stanford, I spotted the Roadrunners. Stretch, the drop-dead-gorgeous-movie-star-hunk, towered over the rest of them. Gus, the curly-haired boy, played the air guitar like he was on fast-forward. The shorter boy with the big smile accompanied him on the trash can as the redheaded boy looked on. Stanford was not among them. Stretch nudged Gus.

"Millie," I whispered. "I think those boys are looking at us. Aren't they Stanford Wong's friends?"

"He has friends?"

I smiled and waved. They huddled, then one of them came toward us. The one Wendy told me to watch out for.

"Hello, ladies," he said. A smile crept across his face. "Let me introduce myself. Digger Ronster, head of the Roadrunners."

"Hi," I said cautiously.

Millie kept her mouth shut.

"Nice song, isn't it?" He motioned toward the couples slowly making their way around the dance floor.

Digger was better-looking up close than from a distance. Handsome, in a weird way. Even though his hair was bright red and his face was covered with freckles, his blue eyes stood out. They were hypnotizing.

He turned to Millicent and I saw her stiffen.

"May I have this dance?" When she hesitated, he murmured, "Come on, let's dance." His voice was smooth.

"No, really . . ." Millicent stepped backward and bumped into me. I held on to her to keep her from falling.

"Let's dance," Digger said, reaching for her hand.

Millie had an odd look on her face that I couldn't read. Digger turned to his friends and gave them a thumbs-up.

"You don't have to go," I whispered, but she was already gone.

As I watched from the sidelines, someone came and stood next to me. It was Stanford Wong! I was afraid that if I looked directly at him I might pass out or, at the very least, hyperventilate. So I tried to look straight ahead. But from the corner of my eye, Stanford looked even better than I remembered. He smelled good too. And his hair! It was a new style and he had the coolest purple highlights. Just to be standing next to Stanford was enough to make me feel like my heart was about to burst from happiness. Nothing could interrupt this moment.

"Get away from me!" Millie yelled as she shoved Digger.

"You're still just a little nerd," he shouted back even louder. "You lost me ten bucks!"

Millie shrank. I started toward her, but Stanford handed me his basketball. He looked angry. "I'll handle this," he said. I moved closer to the dance floor as he made his way to Millicent.

Digger held up his hand to high-five, but Stanford just glared at him.

"Just lost me ten big bucks because this geek-a-zoid here can't dance," Digger complained. "I bet the guys I could get through a whole dance with Miss Smarty-pants."

By now Millicent had covered her face with her hands. I could see Mr. and Mrs. Min through the crowd. They were frozen. So was I. Then Stanford raised his arm and I thought he was going to hit Digger. Instead, he reached out to Millie and offered her his hand.

She just stared at it as if she had never seen a hand before.

"Take it, Millie, take it," I whispered.

After what seemed like a lifetime, she slowly put her hand in his. I wanted to cheer, but instead hugged the basketball even tighter.

"Get lost, loser," Stanford ordered Digger. "Millie knows how to dance, she just doesn't want to dance with you."

Digger looked shocked. "Hey, Stan the Man, can't you take a joke? It's just that I made a bet and then this nerdball . . ."

"And nothing," Stanford said, cutting him off.

Digger paused, then shook his head slowly. "You'll be sorry," he said, scowling. He turned to Millie. "See you around," he snickered before disappearing into the crowd.

Millicent didn't blink. I'm not sure if she heard him.

Still holding hands, Stanford and Millie stood like statues on the dance floor. He said something to her and she nodded. Then they began to dance. They looked awkward, but were talking and smiling in each other's company. After a minute or so, Mr. Min cut in and began to dance with Millicent.

After all that's happened, I would still give anything to dance with my father.

Before I could get too teary-eyed, I spotted Stanford heading back toward me. I didn't want him to see me crying, so I looked up at the sky, hoping the tears would disappear.

"Emily?"

"Oh, hi!" I said, still looking upward.

"I need to talk to you."

My heart raced as I looked at him at last. He didn't look like the confident Stanford I just saw confront Digger.

"I lied about tutoring Millicent," he said, his words tumbling over each other. "It was the other way around."

"Millie explained everything," I assured him.

"She did? And you're okay with it?"

"I will be."

"I hope so. I tried calling you a couple times."

"I know, we have caller ID!"

His face drained of all color.

I couldn't help laughing. "It's okay, Stanford. At first I thought you were being mean. Then Millie explained that you were afraid to talk to me. I thought it was sweet that you kept calling. The only thing sweeter would have been if you actually said something."

"Uh, like what?"

"Gosh, I don't know. How about 'Emily, I'm sorry'?"

"Emily, I'm sorry."

"Nope, too late!"

He looked like his puppy had just been run over. I slugged him in the arm. "Just kidding!"

Neither of us spoke, only I didn't feel awkward, I felt content. As we watched Millie and her dad dance, I tried to think of something meaningful to say. I wanted to tell him that I really missed him and that he hurt me, but I got over it, and that I thought about him all the time, and that I knew from the first time I saw him that we were supposed to be together.

I turned to him and said, "I like your hair. Especially the purple."

"Thanks," he said as he reached for his basketball. For a moment we both held on to the ball.

"Are you two just going to stand there?" Millie barked. "The band left the stage eons ago. Emily, let's go. My dad and I want to go on Monstroso again."

Stanford looked deflated.

"Oh, geez," Millicent sighed. "Okay, Stanford, you might as well come with us. And by the way, *braccae tuae aperiuntur.*"

"Huh?" he said. Millie just smiled mysteriously.

As we waited in line for Monstroso, I tried to figure out how I could sit next to Stanford. Yet even though we rode several times, it was always Millie and me in one car, and Stanford and Mr. Min in the other. Finally, on our fourth or fifth ride, Mr. Min said, "Emily, sorry, but it's my turn to ride with Millie."

I'm not sure who was grinning wider, me or Stanford. The ride operator checked to make sure our seat belts were on tightly. "Scoot over closer to him," he instructed. I could swear I saw him wink at Stanford.

As Monstroso chugged up the long track, I tried not to pass out. Just sitting next to Stanford was causing me to freak out in the best way possible. Finally we reached the top and I had permission to scream.

"Wheeeeeeeeeeeeeeeee!!!!"

"Aaaaaaaaaaahhhhhhhh!!!!"

"Eeeeeeeeeeeeeeeeeee!!!"

"Uh, Emily?"

I was still screaming with my eyes closed. "Whoooooooaaaaa!!!!"

"Emily? Uh, the ride's over," Stanford said.

I opened my eyes. Everyone was staring at me. The ride operator looked amused. Millie looked disgusted.

"I knew that," I sputtered. "I was just goofing off."

Later, after we ditched Mr. and Mrs. Min, Millicent marched ahead as Stanford and I lagged behind. The lights turning on all over the amusement park reminded me of popcorn popping.

"Summer's almost over," I told Stanford.

"Yup, school's starting soon. But at least that means more basketball."

We walked a little bit more. "So you thought I only liked you because you were smart? Exactly how shallow do you think I am?" I tried to look serious, but I was having a hard time keeping a straight face.

"I don't think you are shallow at all," he said as he munched on a piece of peanut brittle. "It's just that, well, I thought that, um, I figured that since you thought I was so smart, you'd hate me if you found out I was dumb."

"Are you dumb?"

"I'm not exactly what you'd call an A student."

"Just because you're not an A student doesn't mean you're dumb." I took the bag of peanut brittle from him and found a really big piece. "I'm not a straight-A student either."

As we navigated through the arcade games, we stopped in front of the basketball bushel throw. Each time Stanford made a basket, my heart fluttered. But that was nothing compared to how I felt when he won a stuffed animal and gave it to me.

"Thank you, Stanford," I murmured as I embraced my elephant. "I'm going to name him . . . Lanford!"

By then it was dark. Millie's parents were waiting for us near the exit. Stanford slowed down. I did too. Finally Millie sighed. "Before we all start walking backward, I'm going to talk to my mom and dad. Emily, meet you there."

I was so glad she could read my mind. Best friends can

do that. If Stanford knew what I was thinking, he would have seen us holding hands.

Stanford and I lingered for a while, not saying anything. Finally he said, "Good-bye, Emily. I had a great time."

"Me too." I hesitated. "Stanford?"

"Yes?"

"Why was Digger so mean to Millie?"

"She embarrassed him big-time once and he's never forgiven her."

"Did he used to throw food at her?"

"Yeah."

"Oh."

"Hey, uh, the Hee-Haw Game's coming up. Will you be there?"

"Hee what?"

"Hee-Haw. It's a basketball fund-raiser. The A-Team plays the teachers and we all ride donkeys."

"Stanford," I said, grinning, "there's no way I'm going to miss that!"

"Emily?"

"Yes?"

"Good night, Emily."

Before I finished saying, "Good-bye, Stanford," I already couldn't wait to see him again.

SEPTEMBER 1

Dear Diary,

After picking up Maddie and her luggage, the Mins and I headed to the gym for the volleyball league awards. I wondered if Stanford would be there. I didn't have to wonder for long. He was sitting in the very back on a top bleacher. When he saw me, Stanford jumped up and waved. Millie's parents and Maddie waved back. I just smiled and nodded.

"Emily! Millicent, over here!" Alice motioned us over to the third row. She was dressed in normal clothes — nice jeans and a polo shirt.

The ceremony was pretty boring. The Serve-ivors placed third out of ten teams. It wasn't what Julie wanted, but I was so happy that I led the team in the "Serve-ivors" cheer.

Later, the teams broke off for individual awards. Wendy looked shocked when she won MVP. Then Coach Gowin said, "The next award is for team spirit. This young lady came to us and totally energized our team with her enthusiasm. Will Emily Ebers please come up?"

I let out a shriek and raced up to receive my award. My very first trophy! Millie and Wendy were on their feet applauding, and then everyone else, including Julie, rose. She even gave me a small smile, and in exchange I gave her a big one.

I could hear Alice cheering the loudest. My face

flushed as I shook Coach Gowin's hand and Mrs. Min took our picture. As I glanced up into the stands, I could see Stanford giving me a thumbs-up.

Then Coach Gowin made one final announcement.

"In a unanimous decision, the award for most improved goes to Millicent Min!"

Millie started crying and so did her father. Her mother handed her a wad of tissues. Maddie whistled so loud that the people near her covered their ears.

Everyone was quiet during the drive to the airport. When it was Maddie's turn to disappear through the security gates, Millie grabbed her and refused to let go.

"You're holding up the line," the guard barked. Reluctantly Millie stepped back.

As Maddie set off the metal detector and the security guards closed in around her, she called out, "Girls, remember your promise!"

Later Millie asked, "What was your promise?"

"She told me to look after you."

"That's funny, she made me promise to look after you too," Millie mused.

After dinner, while I was trying out my trophy in different spots in my room, Alice called out, "Telephone! Emily, it's for you."

"Hello?"

"EMILY!" A.J. shouted. "Wait a minute, I'll get Nicole. Nicole, I've got Emily!"

"EMILY!" Nicole shouted. It was weird because I

didn't recognize her voice at first. "We just got back from camp today. Did you get our letters yet? At camp there was this one counselor, and they found ALL the letters everyone had written hidden under his bed. He was supposed to be mailing them, but he was reading them! Only a couple made it out! But we couldn't understand why we never got any of your letters?"

Then it hit me . . . I never wrote to A.J. or Nicole this WHOLE ENTIRE SUMMER!!! I was so mortified, I couldn't even speak. However, once I got started, I couldn't stop. "Stanford . . . Rialto . . . Millie . . . volleyball . . . hippie . . . tea leaves . . ."

It was just like old times, only everything I said was new; and although I was sharing my summer with them, it was Millicent who had lived it with me.

SEPTEMBER 2

Dear Diary,

I wanted to burn my credit card, but Millie said it was really bad for the environment and "even small gestures like that could add up and contribute to global warming."

There's no way I wanted to get blamed for global warming.

At first I was just going to snip the credit card in half, but once I started cutting, I couldn't stop.

"I hate credit cards, they're so stupid!"

"All credit cards, or just the one your dad gave you?" Millicent asked.

"Can't you just be quiet for once?"

She looked hurt.

"I'm sorry," I said, shaking my head. "When my dad sent this to me, it was really special. He's not big on birthdays."

"Well, what about that limo he hired to take you and your friends into New York City?"

"I've been thinking about that. The limo was full of instruments and speakers. It was for the band, and then he had extra time or something."

"But Emily, he didn't have to take you out for your birthday in a limo. He chose to do that. Nobody forced him. It's called free will. Did you have a nice time?"

"I had a great time."

"So it was a nice present, even if it didn't start out that way."

Leave it to Millicent to logic everything out.

I'm feeling more settled these days. Alice and I are talking a lot. She even took me to meet her psychologist, Dr. Dougherty. Alice was in the room with us, and at first I was scared that if I told her how I really felt about everything, she would get mad or fall apart. But instead, she listened carefully, and any time I hesitated,

Dr. D. would say, "Go on, Emily, it's okay." And it was. It was just like three friends talking, only one was a mom, one was a daughter, and one was a psychologist.

"Well, our time is almost up," Dr. D. informed us. "Emily, did you have anything more you'd like to ask?"

"I do have one more question."

"Go on."

"Do you get paid just for talking to people?"

"I get paid for listening too," she said.

I think I want to be a psychologist when I grow up.

SEPTEMBER 3

Dear Diary,

Stanford and I had made plans to meet at The Scoop before the Hee-Haw Game. I arrived first and as I looked out the window I saw someone running really fast. It was him! The closer he came, the slower he got, until he calmly opened the door and wandered in.

"Hi Emily!"

"Hi Stanford!"

We both blushed. Or maybe he was just all red from running.

"Emily, what flavor are you going to have?"

"I'm not sure, what are you going to have?"

"Uh, maybe something green?"

Stanford turned to the ice-cream lady and said, "We both like green. Is there something special you can recommend?"

He was totally suave. Last night Alice and I watched *Top Cop*. In one scene, Top Cop was trying to impress his date, so he asked the waiter to recommend something special. This was exactly like that!

As she scooped our chocolate mint cones, Stanford reached into his pocket. "This one's on me, only I have to pay cash since I don't have a credit card," he joked.

When he mentioned the credit card, it was as if he had pressed a button. Everything came rushing forward, and there was nothing I could do to stop it. I burst into tears. Stanford looked stricken. He handed me the napkin dispenser, but I shook my head and ran outside. I was happy and horrified when he followed me.

"Emily, is anything wrong? We can get another flavor. It doesn't have to be green. We can get something pink if you want. Or brown? There are a lot of really good brown choices, like chocolate or coffee or . . ."

"My d-d-d-d-dad took away my credit card," I wailed.

"That's okay, I have money. Look." He showed me a crumpled ten-dollar bill.

"It's not that," I tried to explain as I gulped for air. Stanford was still holding the napkin dispenser. I took some napkins and blew my nose. "It's just that the credit card meant something. It was something that my dad gave me and it was important because it was from him. My parents are divorced. It's horrible when your parents don't get along. Oh, Stanford, you have no idea."

"I think I do," he said. By then I was hiccuping.

Stanford put the napkin dispenser down. "Emily, my grandmother gave me something I'd like to show you." He pulled a green jade pendant out from under his shirt. It was on a black cord.

"It's — *hic* — beautiful," I said, sniffing. It really was.

"It brought me good luck for many years," he told me. "Now I want you to have it."

Did I hear him correctly?

"Really? Oh, Stanford, you would — *hic* — give that to me?"

Stanford put it around my neck. I tried not to tremble as I touched the pendant. It instantly calmed me down, like it had magical powers.

"Now I have two beautiful — *hic* — necklaces from my two best friends," I told him, showing him the Millicent necklace, and his.

Stanford was staring at me with a funny look on his face. It occurred to me that boys don't give their good-luck necklaces to just anyone. Maybe I wasn't just anyone to Stanford. Maybe I was more.

"Stanford, does this mean that you are asking me to be your — *hic* — girlfriend?"

When he didn't answer immediately, I panicked.

What if he just wanted to be friends? What if I totally misread everything? What if he thought I was too forward? Was I going to be the first person on Earth to actually die of embarrassment?

"Um, uh, do you want to be my girlfriend?"

I hesitated. "I want to, if you want me to be."

He looked serious before breaking out in the biggest grin I have ever seen. "Then I guess that means 'yes.'"

I couldn't stop smiling. He said, "Yes," he said, "YES!" As I waited for him to do or say something, he came toward me. *He's going to kiss me*, I thought. I was so glad I had practiced on my hand.

Stanford moved closer and closer. It felt like the entire world was moving in slow motion. Then he reached toward me . . . and shook my hand.

I yelped, then surprised both of us by kissing him on the cheek.

He looked shocked — and speechless. But that was okay. His smile said it all.

"You'd better go or you'll be late for your game," I told him. "Look for me. I'll be the one cheering the loudest for you."

Stanford mumbled something, turned around, and walked straight into the wall. I laughed as I watched him weave down the street.

I floated all the way to Stout's where I was supposed to meet Millicent. My hiccups were long gone. All I could think about was the kiss. It was like the first time I had a chocolate-dipped strawberry. Only a hundred billion times better.

"We kissed," I whispered to Millie as I slid into the booth.

"Please, I'm trying to eat my dinner," she said, making a sour face.

Libby came by with a tray full of food and sat down with us. "It's on Maddie," she said. "I was given strict instructions to feed you girls, give myself a break, and send her a bill."

"Do you need permission to sit and eat when you're working?" I asked.

Libby laughed like I had made a huge joke. "Emily, I can do whatever I want. I own the place."

"You own Stout's?" I stammered.

"Well, duh," Millicent said. "Libby Stout. Stout's. Get it?"

I couldn't wait to tell Alice!

Millie was in a wonderful mood. Last night, she found out she's going to be a big sister. She called me after midnight to give me the news.

"I was the first person Millicent told!" I said to Libby.

She raised her water glass and said, "Here's to best friends and big sisters!"

Libby was still sitting in the booth when we left.

"I can't believe you are dragging me to a basketball game played by people sitting on donkeys," Millie muttered as I hurried her along.

"Yes, but I can't miss seeing my boyfriend in the game, can I?"

"I knew that you and Stan-Turd would be boyfriend/girlfriend from the moment you met. There was plenty of foreshadowing," she said smugly.

By the time we got to the gym it was already crowded. I gripped Millie's arm. Rancho Rosetta is so much bigger than Wilcox Academy, and the students looked older and more sophisticated. But even though there were hundreds of people milling around, somehow Stanford spotted us immediately.

"Are you nervous about the game?" I asked.

"Nope." He looked so totally swoon-worthy in his red-and-gold basketball uniform. "It's weird, once I get on the court, I feel right at home. Actually, I feel better than at home. I've never ridden a donkey before, so I'm not sure how that's going to go. And all the other guys are eighth-graders, I'm the only seventh-grader on the team, so I'm hoping they don't reject me, because if they do, my basketball career is in the toilet." He paused. "Uh, I guess I am nervous after all."

When the buzzer rang I screamed. Stanford laughed. He has a nice laugh. "See you after the game, Emily. I gotta go!"

We shook hands, and I watched him run off. I noticed

Julie and the Triple A's staring at me with their mouths hanging open. I turned and saw Wendy in the bleachers with some other girls. She waved to me.

"Want to sit with Wendy's group?" I asked Millie.

"No thanks. They're your friends, not mine. Besides, they don't want to sit with me. You go ahead, though, if that's what you want to do. I'll just sit over here by myself. Alone."

"Stop being ridiculous, Millicent. I want to sit with you. But next time we're both sitting with Wendy and her friends. You need to branch out more."

From our seats I could see everything. The Roadrunners, minus Digger and Stanford, were across from us. Stretch nudged Gus, who stood up and yelled, "Helloooooo, Emily Ebers!"

Stanford must have told his friends about me! I tried to act cool as I waved.

"Don't you think any of them are cute?" I asked Millie.

She hesitated and finally said, "Six at two o'clock, okay? Now leave me alone." That's the highest ranking she's given anyone. It was for the boy named Tico, the short one with the big smile who Wendy says is really nice.

The Hee-Haw Game began with the Teacher Team coming out and acting all goofy. It must be a fun school if the teachers are willing to ride donkeys. Then the A-Team players were introduced one at a time. Stanford was last, and he got the most applause.

Before getting on his donkey, Stanford waved to me. I turned to Millie.

"He just waved at me."

"Wow, what talent."

I have never enjoyed a basketball game so much before. Actually I had never been to a basketball game before. Even so, I knew that something special was happening every time Stanford got the ball. He was really good. No, that's not right. He was really great, and it wasn't just me who thought that.

I wonder what it would feel like to have crowds cheer for you? It must be pretty amazing. I'm sure the Talky Boys had that happen all the time when they were at the top of the charts. I feel bad that Dad's tour didn't end up the way he had hoped. I wonder if he misses the applause?

As Stanford and his team played, I screamed so loud I almost lost my voice. Even Millicent stood up and shouted, although she was rooting for the teachers. At one point she actually shrieked, "Pass the ball!!! PASS THE STUPID BALL, YOU STUPIDHEADS!!!" then immediately slapped her hands over her mouth.

"Well?" I asked when the game was over. The A-Team slaughtered the teachers.

"Statistically, Stanford is an excellent player," Millie conceded.

Just then I spotted Stanford in the center of the crowd.

He pushed his way toward us. "Did you see that last basket I made?"

"Yes, yes, we all saw it, Stanford," Millie said, sounding bored.

"It was spectacular," I gushed, although what I really meant was, "You're spectacular."

When I got home I took out my Stanford Wong Collection and added one Hee-Haw Game ticket stub. But first I wrote on it: "We won."

SEPTEMBER 4

Dear Diary,

I spent the day wandering around Rancho Rosetta. All the places that were so foreign to me a few months ago now felt familiar. Before heading home, I stopped to see Millicent.

"Here, I got this for you," I said, handing her a bag.

Millie opened it cautiously. "What is it?"

"It's a teddy bear of your own. Everyone needs a stuffed animal. I've named him Einstein, but you can change that if you want."

"Einstein," she mused. "Einstein, that's perfect. Thanks, Emily." She gave me a hug.

"You're welcome, Millicent."

Mrs. Min invited me over to dinner, but I already promised Alice I'd eat with her. Millie and I made plans for a sleepover on Friday. Before I left she said, "Emily, I've been giving this a lot of thought. Perhaps your father didn't call you because he couldn't. Perhaps something was holding him back."

"Like what?"

I listened to her theory and nodded.

"You are pretty smart," I said.

"That's what they say," Millicent replied, grinning.

As I headed home, I put a couple of quarters in a parking meter that was about to expire. Old habit, I guess. I wonder if Dad still gets lots of parking tickets? I loved how when I'd race out to feed his meter, he'd say, "That's my girl!"

When I walked into the dining room I was in for a surprise. On the table were two stuffed Cornish hens alongside a three-bean salad and homemade potato latkes with sour cream.

"Are we having company?"

"Nope, just us," said Alice. "I've made chocolate rugelach for dessert too. This is to compensate for all the frozen dinners we've been eating. I think we deserve a feast, don't you?"

As I sat down I realized how hungry I was. I bit into a latke. It tasted better than anything I had had all summer.

I looked over at Alice. She raised her glass. "Here's to new beginnings."

"New beginnings," I echoed as our glasses clinked. *This was as good a time as any*, I thought. "Alice, I was wondering . . . Well, I've been thinking about this for a long time, and I was wondering if . . ."

"What is it, Emily?"

"I was wondering if it would be okay to call you Mom again."

Alice stared at me like I had said something shocking.

"Oh, Emily . . ." her voice cracked. "Of course, of course, honey. I would love for you to call me Mom."

She began to cry, but interrupted herself to say, "Don't worry, these are happy tears."

It was almost bedtime when the phone rang.

"Emily, telephone! It's a boy. Stanford Wong?"

"Mommmm," I said, as she handed me the phone. "May I please have some privacy?!!!"

"Okay, but only talk for ten minutes, then you have to get to sleep."

"Hi Stanford!"

"Hi Emily! Are you ready for school tomorrow?"

"I've figured out what I'm going to wear, but I'm a little nervous."

"Don't be," he said. "I'll be there."

It seemed like we had just started talking when Mom yelled, "Emily, it's been way past ten minutes."

"I have to go now, my mom's on my case. Good night, Stanford."

"Good night, Emily."

"Okay, you hang up first."

"No, you hang up first."

We both waited another ten minutes since we didn't want to be the first one to hang up. Finally we agreed to count to three and then hit the OFF button.

Lanford, TB, and I crawled into the bottom bunk. I hadn't slept there in ages, but Mom wanted to tuck me into bed.

"Stanford Wong?" she asked as I scooted over so she could sit down.

"He's my boyfriend." I was glad it was dark so she couldn't see me blushing.

"Aren't you a little young to have a boyfriend?"

"Mom!" I groaned as I buried my face into Lanford. "I'm not a little kid anymore."

"No, I guess you're not. Just take things slowly, okay?"

"Mother!"

She stroked my hair. "What does Millicent think of Stanford?"

"She thinks he's okay," I said. Though neither will ever admit it, they are good friends. I can see that.

Mom's hair was pulled back in a ponytail and she was wearing her tattered blue bathrobe. She smelled like orange soap.

I remembered when I was little, and how she'd always

check the closet for monsters before tucking me into bed. And then we'd talk and before she left, Mom would always kiss me on the forehead.

I hesitated, then said softly, "Mom, you're never going to leave me, are you?"

"Emily Laura Ebers, I'm surprised you haven't figured it out yet. I'm impossible to get rid of! Sweet dreams, honey."

"Good night, Mom. I love you."

"I love you too, Emily," she said, then she kissed me.

After she left, I turned up the radio in time to hear Lavender murmur, "Perhaps there's someone in your life who can't find their way . . . Here's a song by Cyndi Lauper called 'Time After Time.'"

That's when it occurred to me. I used to feel so lost, but not anymore. I knew exactly who I was and where I was. Just like I knew that my mother would always be there for me, and I would be there for her. And that Stanford Wong would always be my first big crush. And I also knew that despite, or because of, our differences, Millicent Min and I would always be friends.

What I wasn't so sure of was where I stood with my father, and that made me sad.

SEPTEMBER 5

Dear Daddy,

It's after midnight. I've been thinking a lot about something my friend Millicent told me when I left her house tonight. I was really upset earlier this summer when you didn't phone after you returned to New Jersey. But she thinks you didn't call right away because you were embarrassed that the tour didn't work out the way you had planned.

It's funny. We all have these grand ideas about how things should be. And when they don't turn out the way we want them to, we start acting weird or freak out or get paralyzed. I think I did all three this summer. Yet it doesn't have to be that way.

School starts tomorrow and I should be asleep. Instead, I'm writing this letter. I wasn't going to send my journal to you, but I've changed my mind. Even though we are far from each other, I still want to be a part of your life. You don't have to call or write back. But if you ever feel lost or lonely, or just need someone talk to, you know where to find me.

Love always,
Emily

This book was edited by Cheryl Klein and Arthur Levine,

and designed by Elizabeth B. Parisi.

The text was set in Janson Text,

a typeface designed by Nicholas Kis in 1690.

The display type was set in Coop Light & Heavy,

designed by House Industries.

The book was printed and bound at RR Donnelley

in Crawfordsville, Indiana.

The production was supervised by Jaime Capifali.